BIG TROUBLE

An Evelyn Lee Emerson Novel

Denise Jewell

Big Trouble
An Evelyn Lee Emerson Novel

ISBN-13: 978-0692259900
ISBN-10: 0692259902

Editing by: Mary Ann Ellis
Cover Design By: Aeternum Designs
aeternumdesigns.com
Printed format by: Polgarus Studio
www.polgarusstudio.com

DEDICATION

This book is dedicated to my daughter Ebony, without her this book may not have come to fruition. She has been with me and supported me through all of my fears, tears and frustrations. She has been the constant force that pushed me on when I didn't know how to start and when I didn't think I could finish.

To my brother Michael, who told me; "they will and to write it anyway," when I feared people would say bad things about my book.

And to Judge Dwayne Mallory and his wife Beverly Mallory, whose strong black legal family helped to inspire my fiction family.

Prologue

Lying in my bed staring at the ceiling, I think about my life, the person I am, or who I thought I was before "it" all happened. Let me introduce myself so you won't be as lost as I have been feeling as of late. My name is Evelyn Lee Emerson; I'm forty eight years young and I come from a very prestigious black family in Cincinnati, Ohio where I reside with my family. I have been married for twenty- six years to the most wonderful man. He is also a judge; we have four adult children and two grandchildren. I own and operate a travel agency in the bridal district in our town. I have a large, close- knit family that consists of four sisters and two brothers with the corresponding number of in-laws. I also have numerous nieces, nephews, cousins, and of course my lovely parents. My father is a retired judge and mayor; my entire family seems to be in the practice of the law in one form of another. I thought by now I truly knew myself and my family, but when you least expect it they surprise you! Which is where the "it" comes in!

Chapter One

One Month Ago

Walking up the steps in the pouring rain to open my travel agency was not my ideal way to start a new work week. Trying to hold on to my purse, attaché' case, umbrella and cell phone while attempting to unlock the door without dropping anything was like trying to juggle eggs in the snow on roller skates. I've always carried too many things. No matter how many times I said I would get organized before getting in the car from home or getting out of the car at work; either way it never happened. Normally it wouldn't be such a big deal but I was getting soaked in the process. Just as I got the door open while trying to disengage the alarm, the office phone started ringing. Since I was early I could let the call go to the answering machine. Once I finally got the alarm turned off I was able to set my arm- load down so I could put my umbrella away and take off my coat and boots. I've always hated when it rained in the winter; it was already cold, and to add water to the mix was just obscene. I changed my footwear from soggy boots to my nice black leather heels then turned on all the lights in the front and back offices and set the coffee pot to brew in the break room. I love going into the office and being alone in the quiet space before all the hustle. Having my travel business in the bridal district of Reading, Ohio, a tiny city inside of the main city of Cincinnati attracted couples for honeymoons like kids to trick or treating at Halloween. So many people make travel arrangements on line now-a- days with the Internet. It's a good thing that brides want special treatment for their honeymoon, because I'm known for giving them the royal treatment, personalized to whatever they want. They always come back for everything else and recommend others as well. Some people come just because I am an Isaacs by birth and an Emerson by marriage. Being born into one of the most influential black families in the state and then marrying into another makes people want to meet you, if for no other reason than to be nosey. I honestly don't care why they come, as long as I receive their business.

As I sat at my desk drinking my first coffee of the day, I saw my daughter Alicia running in from the rain; right behind her was my daughter- in- law Mia, doing the same mad dash, trying to escape the downpour. They both work for me as my office managers; they came to me right out of college with no managerial experience, so they shared the title. I didn't want to favor one over the other when they both had the same lack of qualifications. So when I came up with the idea of sharing the title of office manager I thought they might balk, but they both were so excited to have the job, they didn't care and they worked excellently together.

Alicia is my third oldest child and second daughter and Mia is married to my only son who is also my oldest. Before my son married Mia I was concerned about the other *women* he brought home and introduced to the family; all I could do was smile to their face and pray behind their backs. I was truly worried about him for a long time. I didn't know what he was thinking; finally my prayers were answered with sweet and pretty Mia, a really nice young lady with proper manners, decorum, and a good attitude.

Now my daughter Alicia, I never had to worry about. Always mature, levelheaded and steadfast, once she has stated what she wants, she goes after it and gets it. In her junior year of college, she set her sights on a man she met on campus one day at some rally or something, the next year they were engaged.

"Good morning ladies!" I said to them as they came from putting away their soaked coats and umbrellas.

"Morning Mama! Morning Evelyn," they proclaimed at the same time.

"Why does it have to be raining like this?" Alicia exclaimed. "You know how it scares me to drive in this mess; it's raining so hard you can barely see. We should have kept the office closed today!" she whined.

I ignored her. She knew better than to think I would close the office for rain, especially with Monday being the busiest day, second only to Saturday.

"Oh Alicia, you know all those brides- to- be will never miss their appointments with us, and the walk-ins will be in as well," Mia said while fixing her coffee. "It's too hard trying to reschedule them all if we closed."

"I know. I just would have rather stayed in bed on a rainy day and slept." Alicia whined some more. I forgot to mention Alicia is a bit of a whiner. Totally my husband's fault!

* * * *

"Mia?" I called out to her in the outer office later that day. I hate to use the phone when I can see them through the glass. Their desks were right outside my office which was in the back; the travel associates and receptionist were in the front office space.

"Yes Evelyn," Mia said as she approached my desk. She knows me; if I called, it meant come here.

"The travel documents arrived for these customers," I said handing her a tall stack. "Pass them out among the associates that have appointments. I don't want the ones that are handling the walk-ins to do it." We always have a continuous stream of walk-ins and they needed to know they were a priority even if they had not made an appointment.

"All right! Your noon appointment is here. I'll send them in. What do you want for lunch?" Mia asked. "It's still pouring, and just like we said the weather didn't stop anyone from making it in to us today, so there's no way we can leave with how busy it is."

"Yes, that would be good. Order Chinese; you know what I like. Thanks, and tell my noon appointment to come in."

Soon after, my appointment, the bride- to- be from hell came in with her mother, and I wanted to send her right back out, but I am Evelyn Lee Emerson and I have an image and reputation to uphold, so of course I put on my professional face and welcomed her into my office again. I don't normally do appointments of any kind but I always handled the richest clients who insisted that only I could handle their travel arrangements. Her name was Melina Simpson; she was cute, and insanely old- money- rich, but she was the most selfish, narcissistic little twit I think I have ever met. She was so consumed with herself that I was convinced she was marrying herself. She never mentioned the groom, only what she wanted and how she wanted it.

"Hello Ms. Simpson, how are you today?" I forced a smile and a false sincerity in my voice.

"Oh Ms. Emerson, I'm doing great. The weather is just awful though, isn't it? Have you gotten all my details together that I want for my honeymoon? I want the stretch limo to pick me up from the airport as well, a white hummer one, of course. And did you remember the strawberries in white chocolate with champagne in the bedroom? I also think I want to hire the housecleaning staff and chef for the entire honeymoon instead of just the first couple of days. I plan to be pampered the entire time."

See what I mean!!? All she does is talk about herself. I swear I will insist she sends me wedding pictures just to prove that I am wrong that she isn't marrying herself. And she never shuts up.

"Umm Ms. Simpson," I tried to jump in while she took a breath, but no such luck.

"Oh, and I also want the bed covered in white and violet- dyed rose petals for when I get there."

"Melina," I snapped. She actually stopped talking, and it seemed as if no one had ever interrupted her from talking because she was truly stunned that I had the gall to do so. At least that's what her facial expression said to me. I waited a moment to see if she would start up again, but no, she still sat there with her mouth hanging open.

"Okay, Ms. Simpson," I said with practiced patience.

"You might as well call me Melina since you already took the liberty," she said with a sarcastic attitude of offense, but not really giving me approval to call her by her first name. I ignored her sarcasm and pretended as if I didn't understand.

"Alright Melina, this is the last appointment to finalize all of both you and your *fiancés* honeymoon plans, and I want to make that perfect for you." She began to smile again. All I had to do was appeal to her narcissism and she was back on track.

"We will go over all the things you already have chosen and then add or subtract anything else. But this will be final because your wedding is coming up soon and I have to make sure everything is absolutely perfect for you." I laid it on thick and she soaked it up. I had her beaming, but of course I did, I was talking about her and I was good at my job. My face was already in pain from my fake smile. How in the world was I going to make it through the rest of the appointment?

Finally I was seeing Melina Simpson and her mother who never talked off, and not too soon either. As a gift to *myself* I promised her that just for her when her travel documents came in I would have them hand delivered. She thought I was the nicest person in the world, but I was just saving my sanity by keeping her out of the office despite her spending thirty grand on a Paris honeymoon. Three more appointments to go before I could go home for the day!

As I was stealing a few moments in the little kitchen in the back of the office eating a late lunch, Alicia came in.

"Mama, Daddy is on the phone for you." This gave me an instant smile. My wonderful Tony, I have loved him it seemed forever. I met him in my father's office twenty-eight years ago this coming summer. I could remember it like it was yesterday! I couldn't believe my eyes at the gorgeous site before me: Six foot three inches of muscle, I could see that under his suit; skin the color of caramel; and light brown eyes looking at me like he thought I was just as breathtaking. That look had made my heart race with excitement. I was twenty and he was twenty-five. He asked me out for dinner that day, and almost twenty-eight years later we are still together and he still makes my heart race.

"Hello." I said to him as I took the cordless from Alicia.

"How's my best lady doing today?" He responded. Ooh, just hearing his smooth deep sexy voice gave me the shakes and he knew it too.

"I'm doing well. Busy Monday as usual, and it's our late day, so a few more appointments until we can close up shop for the day. But how are you today?" I asked.

"I'm good. I just took a break before resuming court, but I'm going to adjourn court at four today. It seems the rain is going to freeze and then we're going to get snow and I don't want to get caught in it, but I don't want you to either. You need to close up early today!"

"You know I won't do that. All the appointments are confirmed, and it's too hard to reschedule them with the already bursting schedule we have. You know I will be careful driving, and if it gets too bad I will stay in that tacky hotel down the road." I made my voice extra sweet so he would agree with me but I really knew better.

"I don't think so," he stated in that firm judge on the bench voice I hated to hear. "If it gets too bad you *will* close early regardless of schedules. They should have more sense than to want to risk their life just to schedule a honeymoon regardless of how good you are or how long it takes to get an appointment with you."

"Fine!" I said sounding like a petulant child. "But only if it starts to get really bad!" I continued promising him.

"Okay, well I have to resume court, I will see you when I get home. Love you!"

"Love you too."

Chapter Two

Finally I was able to leave and the weather held out on me so I didn't have to cancel any appointments. It was still raining but that was okay.

"Alisha, Mia, I'm leaving and headed home," I called out to the girls as I did every evening, leaving them to lock up the office.

"Bye, drive safe," they called in return.

"Oh don't forget that the ladies' vacation meeting is tomorrow," I told them.

"We remember; everything will be ready," Alisha called back to me.

"All right, see you tomorrow." Getting in my car I had to appreciate how much I really loved my husband as I admired my new BMW 760LI that he bought me for my birthday a few months ago. This car was sweet! I was truly blessed with such a loving man. It was amazing that after being together for so long practically nothing had changed between us; we were more in love now than ever. How did I get so lucky? I laughed to myself just from pure happiness. I turned on my favorite radio station and cruised home.

As I turned into my driveway I noticed my father's car parked in front of the house. I wondered what he would be doing here at seven thirty at night. As soon as I walked into the house I heard him right away. My dad talks really loudly and no, he's not hard of hearing. I've known him forty-eight years, my entire life and he's always talked liked that.

"Evelyn, baby girl is that you?" Daddy bellowed.

"Yes, it's me, Daddy!" I called back as I put away my coat. "What are you doing here so late anyway?" I asked him as I gave him a kiss, then walked over and gave Tony one as well.

"Hey baby," Tony said as he squeezed me tight.

"Hi, did you eat already?"

"No, I was waiting to eat with you when your dad showed up; he's only been here about ten minutes."

"Tony, get me some water please while I visit with Daddy for a little bit."

"Sure, I'll be right back," he said as he left the room.

"Daddy, you didn't say what you're doing here at this hour and without Mama and in this bad weather. Is something wrong?"

"No baby girl, I just wanted to get out the house for a little bit and thought I would ride over to see what you and Tony were up to. I hadn't seen you in over a week since I didn't make it to church yesterday."

"Yes, I saw that you weren't there yesterday but since I saw Mama and she didn't act as if anything was wrong, I didn't think anything of it. You okay Daddy; you haven't been feeling bad have you?" I asked worriedly. My parents were really getting up there in age and I didn't want to see them go anytime soon, not at all but that was unrealistic.

"No honey, I was just being lazy and wanted to sleep late. I think after getting to be my age the Lord wouldn't mind me being a little lazy some Sundays."

"Oh Daddy, you can be as lazy as much as you want as long as you stay around." Daddy smiled and patted my knee. He's my favorite parent! I loved my mother, but I'm glad he came without her. She nit-picked everything I did.

"So where's Mama anyway?" Of course I knew she was at home, but being the good daughter that I am I had to ask.

"You can't fool me baby girl, I know you're just asking so I won't think you don't care. I know you love her but I also know you're glad she's not here." We smiled conspiratorially at each other. He had my number. Boy did I really love my daddy!

"No, your mother was on the phone talking to one of your sisters when I left, and she's fine," Daddy continued.

"Daddy, do you want something to eat? Today was my late day at the agency. I'm starving, and Tony hasn't eaten either."

"No, I'm fine but I will come and sit at the table with you both if you don't mind."

"Of course not, come on in the kitchen." I got up and he followed me into the kitchen. There Tony was holding my bottle of water; I wondered where he had gone but I saw that he was talking to our youngest daughter Alexandra. When she saw us enter, she stopped and ran to my dad for her hug and kiss.

"Granddaddy!" She exclaimed, "I didn't know you were here. What are you doing here?" Everyone loved my daddy; he was such a lovely, loud man.

"Oh I'm just visiting your mama and daddy for a spell. What are you doing?" Daddy asked her.

"Nothing. Just talking to Daddy before I head up to my room. I still have some more studying to do for a test tomorrow."

"Oh that's good. You do that so you can be that wonderful lawyer I know you will be," Daddy said proudly to her.

"In this family do I even have a choice?" Alex asked in a joking voice. "Not one of my classmates has a family of lawyers and judges but me; I have a lot to live up to."

"Honey!" Daddy said to her, "You only have to do your best. Don't think about me or your daddy or anyone else. Just know that you have your family supporting you and a great firm to join when you're finished."

"I will Granddaddy; I promise. Well, I'm going to say goodnight now. I'm sure you'll be gone when I make it back down later on."

"Goodnight, sweetheart. Study hard," Daddy told her.

While Alex had been talking with Daddy, Tony had warmed our food and we'd begun eating.

"Alex," I called to her before she could get away. "If I don't get these shoes off my feet I'm going to go crazy, take my shoes upstairs and bring me my house shoes please. I'm going to stay down here with Daddy and talk." She grabbed my shoes and ran up the back stairs. She was back in less than a minute; she never did anything at normal speed. "Thank you baby, but be careful on those steps, you always make me so nervous," I chastised her.

"Mama, I'm fine. Good night," she called out to all of us as she ran up the stairs again.

"Daddy, you sure you don't want anything to eat or drink?"

"No, I'm fine. You continue to eat. So how's your travel agency doing?"

"Business is great as usual. Praise God. Still dealing with those crazy brides- to- be, but they keep me in business. Tomorrow we have our LV meeting."

"What's an LV meeting?" He asked.

"You know Daddy, the meeting with all my sisters and sisters-in-laws to discuss our winter girls getaway."

"Oh I remember now. So where are you going this time?"

"This year it's Gatlinburg, Tennessee. But we have to decide if we are going to stay at a chalet or the ski resort. It really doesn't matter to me, but tomorrow we have to decide. I already put a hold on both since they go fast but the final decision must be made."

"Who's all going?" Tony asked.

"Same as last year as far as I know, except Janice isn't going this time." I said clearly sounding disappointed.

"Janice isn't going?" Tony asked in surprise.

"No, and I really wish she were," I said sounding glum. "I'll mention it to her again and see if I can change her mind in the morning."

"We'll finalize everything tomorrow."

"Have you talked to Jackie lately?" Daddy asked me.

"I usually talk to her every other day or so, but now that you mention it I haven't talked to her since last Wednesday or Thursday. Any particular reason why?"

"She's been over to the house quite a bit lately and though I'd love to see her all the time this is unusual for her and she seems a bit down."

"Has she said anything?" I asked.

"No. I asked, but she said she was fine, she just had new ideas for a charity event to discuss with your mother and preferred to come over. Now, you know she never comes over to do that."

My sister Jackie and my mother sponsored and ran numerous charity events as well as sat on boards of one kind or another, and

Daddy was right they either talked on the phone or at the office. Jackie usually went over to the house once a week to just visit.

"She usually tells me most things and she hasn't said anything at all. So I wouldn't worry too much about it, but if I notice anything I'll ask her about it," I told Daddy hoping to reassure him.

We sat in the kitchen talking until nearly ten at night when my mom called to tell my dad it was time for him to come home. "Good night Daddy. Call as soon as you get home to let us know you made it safely." I gave him a hug and kiss. "Tony will walk you out." I went upstairs to our bedroom as Tony walked my daddy outside to his car.

I was getting into the shower in our en suite bathroom when I heard Tony enter our room. As I stood under the spray I realized just how tired I was; I really needed to get in bed. Just thinking about my meeting with my sisters the next day was enough to drain me. We all got along really well, but trying to get so many different women to agree on something was sometimes so exhausting. People thought we were the weird siblings because we never fought growing up.

My daddy always said, "Never fight your own family," and "We stick together no matter what." What people didn't know was that fighting and arguing wasn't worth the punishment my daddy put us through. If he caught us arguing he would make us write out an argument like we were lawyers in court and we had to present our arguments to the judge, which of course was Daddy. We had to keep our mouths shut until it was our turn, and sometimes we actually had to continue our court sessions into the next day and give a closing argument. Who in their right mind would want to argue when they had that to go through?

We learned our lessons the hard way. So, by the time I was about sixteen there was no more not getting along; we made it work and worked it out. The weirdest part of all with my sisters was that we didn't just resemble one another, we looked nearly just alike. It was on the spooky side, people said. To us and our family we looked like our individual selves but to people who didn't know us, they would swear that they saw one of us at a certain store but of course it was another sister. We're all around the same size and height as well, except for Ava, my baby sister, who was short like our mother. Apparently we looked like Dorothy Dandridge, a black movie star from the silver screen days of Hollywood, but we liked that compliment because she was the epitome of gorgeous.

Feeling like I was dragging a dead man, I was so tired going through my nightly routine, I practically dove for the bed as soon as I was finished. I was under the covers and asleep so fast I didn't feel Tony put his arm around me as he'd done every night for twenty- six years.

Chapter Three

I woke up refreshed and forced myself to make my morning run on the treadmill since it was so cold and seemed to have snowed more overnight. I didn't like running on the treadmill though, I always felt like I was going to fall off and bust my face. Thank God I never did. And running on a treadmill was boring; I liked running outside with real scenery. Tony ran every morning as well, but he ran much earlier since he was up and gone before I woke up most mornings. Once showered and dressed, I went downstairs to the kitchen where our housekeeper Janice, who was also my best friend, was cooking breakfast.

"Good morning Janice! How are you today?" I said to her.

"Good morning to you too Evelyn, I'm just dandy on this cold Tuesday morning. You seem pretty chipper yourself." Janice glanced and smiled at me while she fried bacon at the stove.

"I just made a fresh pot of coffee. Tony drank half the pot before he even had his breakfast. He never drinks that much, but I guess he was tired. You've been keeping that good man up late?"

"You know how he is," I said. "He's always watching something late on TV. I was asleep before my head hit the pillow" I poured myself some coffee and sat down at the table for our morning chat.

"Why were you so tired last night?" Janice asked as she started scrambling the eggs to go with the bacon.

"I really don't know. It was my long day at the office but that's nothing new. Daddy came over and we sat talking to him for a while and it got a bit late, for me anyway, so I guess that was it."

"What was your daddy doing over here so late for?"

"Oh, he said he was missing me since we didn't see one another at church on Sunday and I hadn't been over. I need to go over and visit more often."

"Yes you do. Your parents don't need to be driving in this weather at their age nor late in the night either. Be a good daughter." She chastised me as she handed me my plate of bacon, eggs, grits and toast. "I am a good daughter, I'm Daddy's favorite, remember."

"I know you are. Well you and Ava, but that's because she's just like you and you're both just like him so he overlooks whatever the two of you do."

"He does not. We don't do anything. We're too old to do anything; I'm a grandmother, you know." I smiled mischievously at her.

"Pfft!" She said to me. Sometimes I thought Janice knew me better than I knew myself. She has been our housekeeper for almost as long as I've been married, and she was only ten years older than I was. I was a bridesmaid at her wedding when she married her husband John and she had always been a great friend. She was so pretty: she was medium height and plump, with a small roundish- shaped face, large brown eyes and thin lips, and she wore her hair in a short, stylish cut. She always wore colorful running suits and white athletic shoes to work; she probably owned every color that existed in those suits. I once tried to track all the different colors, but I didn't know the names of all the shades so I gave up.

"Janice, I wish you were coming on this vacation with us. We always go on trips together. You're my road dog; I think that's what it's called," I said laughing.

"I know. But with Sophia's tuition, having to get the furnace fixed, and trying to save for the trip John and I are planning, it's just too much right now."

I stared at her in disbelief; I couldn't believe what she had just said. She needed something and had not told me.

"Janice, do you need money? Let me just grab my checkbook," I said turning to leave the kitchen in search of my purse.

"Evelyn, no!" she said a little sharply, stopping me before I made it out the kitchen door." I'm sorry. I didn't mean to sound harsh but you don't need to loan us any money. We're fine. It's just that needing to replace the furnace was unexpected. Things are fine. Doing anything extra right now is just out of the picture," she explained.

I was hearing her and I understood, but I didn't like it. Ninety nine percent of the time Janice came along, but I guess this was the one percent when she wasn't going to be.

"Okay then, if you're sure you don't need anything!" I pressed. "You promise you will tell me if you do."

"You know I will," She promised me.

As I finished my breakfast I remembered I hadn't told her about the cleaners. "Oh, will you make sure you take all those clothes I put in my bedroom chair to the cleaners today instead of tomorrow? I want to wear that navy and silver dress for the dinner party we have to attend tomorrow evening, and I want to make sure it gets back in time," I said to her as I got up from the table and walked through the kitchen door. "And have the purse cleaned too." I had to yell; by this time I had made it to the front hall and was putting on my boots and coat. "Bye!" I called out. "Call me if you need anything." I have no idea what she said back to me, but if it was more important than goodbye she would have to call me on the phone.

Back in the office later today I was preparing for the LV meeting in our conference room in the back. "Mia!" I called out to the front. "Has lunch gotten here yet?" I catered a full lunch from a great steak restaurant called Ebony's Bar and Grill that had been open for a few months now down on the river.

"They just drove up this second," Mia called back.

"Okay, thanks."

Once lunch had been set up and the delivery drivers had left, my sisters started to come in one by one, no more than five minutes apart. I was surprised! Adele, my oldest sister, was always late everywhere she went, but she walked right in behind our sister-in- law Sheila. I soon found out why she was on time.

"I drove us both here," Sheila proclaimed when she noticed the surprised look on my face upon seeing Adele.

"Oh," we all said at the same time.

"What?" Adele said in an offended tone of voice. "You all act like I'm never on time."

"You're not! That's why I insisted I pick you up; we get tired of waiting on you all the time," Sheila said to her.

"Ladies, no arguing today," My sister Jackie said to them. She was always the mediator of our group, forever the diplomat, the calm one. And thank God for her because I know that definitely was not me.

"Okay ladies, let's sit down and eat so we can move on and get these details finalized." I said as I sat down at the head of the table.

My sister Ava was immediately to my left. Though I had four sisters, if I did have a twin Ava would be it; she looked just like me with the exception of being shorter and younger than I. We had also both inherited that no-boob gene from our mother. (None of us had much in that department but our wonder bras were our best friends). Thank God we had hips and butt, or we would be in sad shape. My other sister Gwen, who was to her left, was Adele's twin in nature but was the quieter of the two. If Adele was involved, Gwen was as well. They handled most of their legal cases together too. Sheila, my sister-in-law, was to her left. Whoever wrote the song "She's A Bad Mama Jama" that Carl Carlton sang had to have been thinking of Sheila because she's the epitome of "built and stacked" with a face to match and skin the color of milk chocolate. A true beauty: my brother hit the jackpot when he landed her, and you couldn't hope for a better person to have around. On my right was my other sister-in-law Katherine. She was a mousy, no-backbone-woman who spent her life doing whatever my brother told her to do and baking cookies. Thank God my brother was a good man because if he wasn't, her picture would represent the definition of doormat in the dictionary. Though physically she was nothing like Adele because where Adele was tall and thin Katherine was short and a bit on the heavy set side, they both were always dressed to the nines no matter the occasion. Katherine was a homemaker, but she arose bright and early every single day and dressed and put on her makeup as if she were going to work or some social event. That, though, is where Katherine's similarities ended with, well, everyone. When my brother Duncan brought her home many decades ago we were confused as to where he found her; she was attractive, but she was the exact opposite of all of the females in his own family. It was like he went out of his way to find someone completely unlike us. And since he had, it took her a while to get comfortable with our outspoken group. Next to Katherine, my sister Jackie was on her right, Jackie was my heart; she was my favorite though I think I hid it well. We were kindred spirits. She was also always on those trips that Janice and I took. My oldest sister Adele was to her right; you know how some men are considered to be true alpha males? Well if Adele was a male she would be an alpha. She was always in charge and got her way; she was a leader, a pit bull in the courtroom and image was everything.

Adele was still upset and shooting daggers at Sheila for speaking the truth. I know she wanted one of us to say something in her defense, but Sheila was right and we all knew it, so we ignored Adele's indignation. Adele was also very spoiled so sometimes, like now, she acted beneath her age. Adele was fifty one years old; she was never going to change so we lessened her influence by changing the game at times, thus not letting her drive.

As we finished up lunch I thought it was now time to get down to business. "Everyone, I've put together a packet of information on the two places I thought that fit our needs best. Sheila, would you hand out those packets down at the end of the table?" I asked her as I pointed to the stack closest to her.

"I'll do it!" Adele jumped out of her chair and grabbed the stack of folders before Sheila could take action or say a word. I noticed and I'm sure the others did as well, but Adele had decided to keep her attitude and to act like a child in a grown woman's body. I swear the older she gets the more childish she becomes at times. What are grandmothers coming to now-a-days!!

After Adele passed out the folders and had retaken her seat, I began. "In the folder you will see the two that I chose. On the left side I chose the actual ski resort, Deer Oak Ski Resort, and on the right side, Snow Mountain Chalets. They are both excellent as far as their amenities and really the only difference is privacy and price. At the chalet we get total privacy but still only a ten minute drive to the ski resort as well as only a few miles from downtown Gatlinburg."

"What's the difference in price?" Ava asked.

I explained the difference in price for the resorts and the chalets. Both were luxurious; we receive plenty of extras with both. The prices were high but we had paid more before.

"I like the idea of the chalet because of the privacy," Katherine said.

"Me too!" Gwen and Jackie spoke at the same time.

"Well, what do we get for all that money?" Adele asked snidely. "That's a lot of money and my money does not grow on trees."

My eye started to twitch. If I were violent or raised by different parents, I would slap my sister. Everyone knows we are truly blessed financially and right this very moment from what I could see, since she was sitting away from me, she had on a black cashmere sweater and black jeans. If I remember correctly from when she walked in, she had on black riding boots, her gold Cartier bracelet that cost thirty five thousand dollars, gold earrings and carried her Valentino purse that I knew cost over two grand. Between clothes, shoes and jewelry, Adele was wearing about fifty thousand dollars, and she dressed like this every day of her life. I have no idea why she was pretending money was an issue or that any of the prices I gave were expensive to her. I just answered her question as if she weren't being a horse's ass.

Adele was truly *high* maintenance; the rest of us were just maintenance! "There are eight bedrooms, eight baths, eight Jacuzzi tubs, hot tub, gourmet kitchen with sub zero refrigerator, all stainless steel appliances, gas grill, home theater room, and game room. The kitchen seats twenty people and free Wi-Fi, and they included three separate hour-long helicopter tours for us and skiing lessons. There are some other things like massages as well, but you can read them in the packets that were passed out to you." Everyone "oohed and aahed" over the amenities.

"I suppose that is a good price for the money," Adele conceded.

"Basically," I continued," the ski resort gives us the same thing for a lesser price , minus the helicopter ride and we will have to share the common areas and we won't have our own hot tub and grill. Things like that."

"Having a travel agency, I was able to put a hold on both places. But, we need to decide which one so I can cancel the one we don't want," I added.

"Well, before we decide aren't we going to bring another person so it will be an even number of people?" Ava asked.

"Yeah, I thought you were going to get an eighth person," Sheila said.

"I didn't know who to ask. Janice is going away with John soon so I didn't want to ask her to shell out any more money in a short amount of time." I would never tell them anything about Janice's personal finances.

"Hmmm"… Ava sighed.

"Well, I could ask Anne," Jackie said.

"Anne? Who is Anne?" Gwen asked.

"She's Michael's sister," Jackie answered. Michael is Jackie's husband, but since she was Jackie's sister-in-law we didn't know her. We had met her a few times over the years but she was a part of Jackie's other family not ours so we didn't really know her.

"That's fine with me if she wants to go." I said. "Everyone just write me a check for your eighth. If she wants to go just tell her to pay me her portion, and if she doesn't want to go, you can ask someone else. But I will pay the other portion if we can't get anyone else to go." I told Jackie.

"But we still haven't decided. I think from everyone's responses that you want the chalet, but let's take our vote. All that want the ski resort raise your hand!" I looked around the table and no one had their hand up.

"All who want the chalet raise your hand." Everyone raised their hands smiling. "Great," I said as I clapped my hands joyfully. "That is a unanimous vote for the chalet."

"We are leaving in four weeks; how are we going to get down there?" Adele asked me.

"We're driving. But, who are we driving with and what, I don't know but I'll take any suggestions."

"How about we rent one of those mini-buses with like twelve or so seats," Ava suggested.

"That's a good idea;" they were all saying.

"I'll drive it," Sheila said.

"Well, that was easy," I said. "I'll have Alicia or Mia look into those and renting one. We'll grocery shop when we get there. "Oh, I forgot the price of the chalet also includes skiing lessons for all of us for four days, so everyone needs to buy a ski outfit." Everyone eagerly agreed. I just think it was because it gave them all a reason to go shopping.

After about thirty more minutes of talking, everyone started to leave, but I noticed Jackie was hanging back and I knew without asking she wanted to talk to me in private. "Jackie, let's go to my office; the chairs are more comfortable in there," I said as I led the way to my office and plopped down in my chair. "So what's on your mind sister dear?"

"I wanted to talk to you about Anne since I said I would ask her."

"Shoot!"

"Well, if she can go, I will pay for her portion on everything. I just didn't want you calling her asking for payment; and I didn't think anyone else needed to know. I don't really know what's going on. I just know things have not been good for her in a while, something to do with her husband." Jackie told me in a dour tone.

"Okay, of course I won't say anything to her about it. I'd never want to embarrass her, just let me know if she's going or not. You have any idea what's going on with her and her husband at all?" I pushed for a little bit more info. I could be nosey; I can admit that about myself.

"No," Jackie said. "She just stopped coming around and calling. I asked Michael about it, but you know men, and him especially. He just shrugged his shoulders in that way of telling me he had no clue, and it wasn't his business." And Jackie is not like me. She would just let Michael get off with just a nothing answer. Tony would never get away with that with me; he knew better.

"Will you be at the Kennedys' dinner party tomorrow?" I asked her.

"Yes. But I really don't want to go. But it's important to support the firm as well as the family." She was referring to our family's law firm. Her husband Michael was not a lawyer but a CPA, and he handled many of our families' multiple businesses as well as many other accounts for other businesses around the city. His company was in the same building as the firm. My daughter Alicia's husband Benjamin works as a junior accountant in his firm.

"Well, I'm going to head on home now," Jackie told me as she stood to put her coat on.

"All right, don't forget to let me know if Anne is coming with us."

"Will do! Bye ladies."

"Bye, Aunt Jackie," Mia and Alicia called out as she walked past their desk towards the door. I only then remembered to ask her if something was going on with her!

Chapter Four

I finally got home around seven-thirty again that evening after a long and fairly uneventful day and the house was quiet and peaceful as usual. As I walked into the bedroom, I saw Tony lying on the bed watching TV. "Hello," I said to him as I walked over and gave him a kiss.

"Hi baby!" He said back to me as he kissed me. He pulled me down on top of him and I screamed from surprise.

"Hey," I said while laughing. "Where did that come from?"

"I miss my woman; you've been working too much. You're always so tired lately when you get home and you just eat and go to bed. I want some lovin'!" He was kissing me as he was saying all of this.

"Oh really," I said, kissing and still laughing at the same time. "Well, let me get undressed, you impatient man."

"You don't need to get undressed; I can do that for you myself." And he proceeded to do so.

A while later we lay in bed cuddled together. "I need to get up and get something to eat. You attacked me as soon as I got in the door you know."

"I attacked you, did I?" he asked as he squeezed me tight.

"Yes, and I loved it, but now I need to eat. What did Janice cook for dinner today?"

"She didn't. I told her I would order something so I picked up barbecue on the way home for us."

"That's fine, let me get washed up and changed and I will go down and eat."

"Don't you dare. I will go and bring it up for you, and we will watch TV and relax." Tony stared at me. "I meant what I said. I think you are working too much. I think you need to stop working the late days."

"But!" I tried interrupting him.

"But nothing. Evelyn, I don't want you wearing yourself out. I don't like seeing you so tired all the time. Not getting home until eight most nights, eating late, just falling into bed, then opening the agency again the next morning," he spoke in exasperation.

"But I love my work," I told him.

"I know you do, but you don't need to kill yourself to do it. You've been working so much lately you haven't even been over to see your parents in weeks." He had me there, and he knew it. And I did feel guilty about it, but he didn't have to make me feel worse than I already did.

"I know, and I promised myself I would go over to visit on Friday after work and I would go after church on Sunday too. Now stop harassing me and go get my food please," I said as I closed the bathroom door.

When I came out of the bathroom Tony was in the sitting area of our bedroom where he had set up a tray with my dinner on it. "Thank you!" I told him.

"Come here," He held out his hand to me. As I took it, he stood up and I had to look pretty far up to look in his face. I was five foot-five and Tony was six foot-three.

"I'm not trying to boss you, you know that right?" I shrugged. "I know you. And if your parents died, you would feel so guilty, you would cry about not visiting them like you should have."

"Tony stop! Are you happy now? Knowing you're right?" I said to him with definite attitude.

"Sit down and eat your dinner!" He said to me, ignoring my attitude as he went and swiveled the TV around to the sitting area and sat next to me.

"Anyway," he said. "How was your day?"

"My day was very good actually. We had the LV meeting and it went surprising smoothly. Adele was trying to be a pain as usual, but even with her, being her, it still went well. And Jackie is going to ask her sister-in-law Anne if she wants to go to even out the number."

"That sounds nice," Tony said.

"She said that Anne was having problems at home and that she would pay for her portion, which is fine with me. It's not my business who pays for what; I just take the money."

"Well, I guess she was worried you might say something to Anne."

"That's what she said. But I couldn't imagine what I could or would possibly say. Anyway, she said she didn't know what their problems were. You know I tried to find out but no such luck." Tony laughed, he always did when he found out my nosiness didn't pan out, and I was disappointed.

"Tony?"

"Hmmm?" He was into whatever was on TV.

"I'll think about what you said regarding cutting back my hours." He turned to me and kissed me.

"Thank you," he said. "That's all I ask," And he went back to being sucked into whatever program he was watching.

The next morning as I came down for breakfast, I heard Janice ending a phone call. "Good morning!" I said to her.

"Good morning to you. That was Anne. She said she was Jackie's sister-in-law and that she would bring her money to you at your agency sometime this morning."

"That's odd; Jackie said she would be paying for Anne's portion herself."

"Well, maybe Jackie gave her the money to give to you; you know how thoughtful Jackie is. She would want Anne to feel like everyone else in your eyes, since you're in charge of everything," Janice said.

"I suppose. But I just accept the money. I'm starting to get confused on who does what, and what I can and cannot say. All Jackie had to do was give her the money and never say anything to me regarding her home problems."

"Home problems! What kind of home problems?" Janice asked as she handed me my breakfast plate.

"I have no clue; all Jackie said to me was she was having problems at home."

"Well, she seemed like a nice lady when I was talking to her on the phone. I hope everything works out for her," Janice said.

"Janice, get a cup of coffee and sit down with me. I'm taking my time this morning. Alicia's going to open up for me today."

"I guess I will sit down and enjoy a cup with you; it's been awhile since we have had a morning cup together and just talked."

"Lately you're only in here long enough to eat and run. We barely see one another anymore." Apparently I was getting too busy for everyone. When had that happened?

"I know and I miss it too!"

"Tony says he wants me to slow down and stop working the late days, that it makes me too tired."

"He loves you Evelyn," Janice said to me seriously.

"I know he does but it's my business and I love it."

"Did he say you should quit?" She asked me.

"No, he'd never do that."

"Well then, he just said slow down and I agree with him. He probably wants you to spend more time with him as well. All your kids are grown and busy. It's time for you to focus on him."

"I do focus on him; I love him more than anything. You know that!"

"Listen to me. I'm not trying to disrespect you or get in your personal business. I do know how much you love him, but I also see him when he gets home and you're never here. He really misses you; and a wife needs to be home to greet her husband at least sometime."

Maybe she was right, I thought. Tony and I always talked about all the things we would do together when the kids got big and now we had no more actual "kids" and I was working all the time.

"Well," I said. "Tony understands how important my business is, but I will ask him how he feels, if it's more than his concern over me being tired."

"Good, you do that!" Janice said. "You've been with that man over half your life. Think about what he's not saying, not just what he is saying."

"Okay, I promise to do that." I had to promise or she might not ever shut up.

"But what's going on with you? How is Sophia doing?" Sophia was Janice's daughter and though Janice was on sixty's door, her daughter was only twelve. For years she and John couldn't have children and had long given up. Then one day at the age of forty-five she was pregnant for the first time.

"Oh, she's doing great. She graduates sixth grade this year and I want to give her a party. I know most don't do sixth grade graduation parties."

"Oh come now," I interrupted. "There is nothing wrong with giving her a party for anything you want to give her a party for, and it is a graduation after all. I will come if more than little kids will be there, and I'll buy her a present. Just let me know what she wants."

"You don't have to do that. You already give her birthday and Christmas presents."

"I know I don't have to, but I want to, I love Sophia, she's like another niece so I don't want to hear any more about what I don't have to do," I scolded her sweetly. "Just remind me when you decide on the date. That's a few months away there is no way I will remember by then."

"I will; let me get up from this table, I have lots of work to do around here today. Oh, the cleaners said your clothes would be delivered this afternoon, but the dress you're planning to wear tonight wasn't dirty."

"Yes, I know but I wanted to make sure it was fresh since I hadn't worn it in about six months."

"Well, I will have everything laid out for you in your dressing room so you won't have to go running around looking for anything."

"You know me so well." I said smiling at her.

"Yes I do," She said with a bigger, smug smile.

Chapter Five

The next evening at the dinner party I stood talking to Madeline Kennedy at whose house we were. I couldn't stand her but I wasn't allowed to show it; being the wife of a judge and the daughter of a retired mayor and judge, I could never publicly show my dislike of anyone. I was raised to play kissy- kissy, nice-nice with the best of them, so I put on the best fake smile I could. Madeline was the kind of person who made you feel like she was competing with you when you didn't even know there was supposed to be a contest. She always had to tell you how much money she paid for something. At the same time never telling where exactly she bought something if you even hinted at wanting to know. She wasn't anything to look at either, or rather she was, but not in a good way. She was white and pale; and when I say white, and I mean white; and so pale that if she weren't standing here talking to me I would swear she belonged in a casket. She was so pale she resembled a corpse including the pancake make-up those funeral homes used. She was tall and skinny as a rail which just added to the corpse theory if you asked me but no one was.

"Oh Evelyn, will you be at the Silver Ball Gala next month?" Madeline asked me.

"No, I…" I began but as soon as I started talking she continued.

"It will be just wonderful I know! I flew all the way to New York so I could shop. I bought just the most beautiful full length gown just for the event, and matching shoes and clutch and I got them all for a steal; I only spent about sixty- five hundred dollars."

"WOW, Madeline, that's great! Where did you shop?" I couldn't care less, but at these functions you played the part.

"Oh you know, all over. There are so many department stores and boutiques there, and since this is *the* gala of the year I thought a trip there to buy my gown was worth it. I just can't believe you aren't going to be there." I couldn't believe she had heard the no when I said it.

"Well, Tony and I will be out of town this year." That was a lie. In truth, Tony and I would be sitting at home watching television; we just didn't want to go, but that was our little secret. Madeline droned on.

"Well you're going to wish you hadn't missed it. All the best people will be there." Oh, she's a snob as well.

"You know Madeline, we are a bit upset that we'll miss it," I lied some more. "We just have to be gone this time, but there are so many other events to attend later this year."

"Mother!" We both turned towards the voice calling Madeline. It was her daughter Brittany coming towards us. She was a very pretty young woman, with long dark brown hair, nice hazel eyes, and full lips. She was tall and hippy but shaped very nicely. I think her father is Greek or something but he blessed her with great coloring and apparently her body as well; she didn't resemble death at all. I remembered she had gone to school with my children, had been on the cheerleading squad with my daughter Olivia, and had her sights on my son TJ for a while. I'm so glad my son did not end up with her; there was no way I could have spent shared family dinners with her mother.

"Hello, Mrs. Emerson, it's good to see you." Brittany said giving me a quick hug.

"Hello Brittany, it's good to see you too. How are you doing?" I said returning the hug.

"Oh, I'm doing great, just adjusting to married life."

"I understand. It's been a long time for me but I still remember those early days." I said in a knowing tone. We all laughed!

"Excuse me Mrs. Emerson, but I need to borrow my mother." Thank God I thought.

"Of course, Madeline I will see you later. It was good seeing you again, Brittany."

"Same here," she said as she and Madeline walked away. At that moment Jackie walked up with two champagne glasses in her hand with a knowing smirk on her face.

"I thought you could use this," she said to me as she handed me the glass.

"Why didn't you rescue me? She's had me tied up for thirty minutes talking about shopping in New York and how much she spent on her outfit for the *Gala of the Year*," I said in a hoity-toity voice trying to mimic Madeline. Jackie started giggling and then giggling and then giggling some more. People were beginning to stare, including me.

"What in the world is so funny?" I asked her. She was giggling uncontrollably.

"I don't know." She was trying to stop and get her breath. "You just seemed so funny mimicking her. I pictured her saying it like that and all of a sudden I couldn't stop laughing." She was still trying to stop laughing.

"Jackie, are you drunk?"

"Maybe!" She said giggling some more.

"How many drinks have you had?"

"Not that many." Mmm hmmm, I thought. I didn't believe that for a second. As I paid closer attention she had that glassy-eyed look of the drunk or tipsy and we hadn't had dinner yet.

"Jackie, where is Michael?" I asked as my eyes searched him out in the crowded rooms.

"Michael is in the other room talking to judge or councilman somebody; I really don't know or care. All of these parties are the same, all the people the same," she said, her words beginning to slur. She was right though about these dinner parties. This was one of the larger ones though, since Madeline and her husband had one of those old mansions with an actual ballroom, which was where the actual dinner would be held. They had a very elegant home, decorated in gold and crème colors throughout. The furniture was in that style that said class but not comfortable, and there were very nice paintings in every room.

"Come on Jackie." I grabbed her arm and steered her towards a buffet of hors devours; she needed something on her stomach. "Here, eat some of these crackers and cheeses," I told her. She obeyed, thank goodness. I don't know what I would have done if she had given me a hard time in her state. Just then I saw my sister Ava and her husband Charles and tried to casually wave and get their attention. I don't think I pulled off casual; I looked more like I was ducking and diving.

"Ava!" I whispered loudly. Ava jerked her head in my general direction upon hearing her name called. She obviously saw me doing my duck and dive move as I gestured her over to us. She was smiling at me with a confused what's-going-on face as she walked towards me.

"Evelyn, you look like some goofy jack- in- the box." Ava said still with the questioning look.

"I do not!" I had to defend my honor. "Anyway," I told her exhaling a deep breath. "Your sister is a bit tipsy with nothing on her stomach." As I swung my gaze back to Jackie she had gotten another glass of champagne from the passing waiter and was throwing it back.

"Jackie, what are you doing?" I took the glass from her but I was too late; it was empty. "Ava, stay here while I go and get Michael to take her home."

"No, don't go get him." Jackie grabbed my hand and stopped me. "I'm fine, this dinner is important for his business." I didn't understand her. She knew this dinner was important but she was still getting sloshed and in front of his colleagues! However, this was not the time nor place to have a heart to heart with her.

"Ava, what do you think?" I asked her.

"I'm not sure," Ava replied as she stared at Jackie with her lips turned up.

"Jackie, what's going on?" Ava asked her.

"There's nothing going on; I just wanted a drink. I didn't think about how much but I'm fine."

"This is what I'm going to do." I said in a sober tone. "I'm going to just tell Michael what's going on, well as best as I can describe this, but also to let him know you're fine."

"So why tell him at all?" Jackie slurred.

"Because, he's your husband and he needs to be on guard. I'll be right back; Ava, watch her." I turned around and walked into the crowd before she could stop me this time. I knew Ava wouldn't let her go anywhere just in case. I saw my other two sisters and their husbands and my brothers and their wives. We saw one another more at these social engagements than we did at our own family functions. As I went in search of Michael it seemed everyone wanted to stop me and talk; I didn't want to appear rude but I was on a mission. I don't know what had gotten into Jackie; she didn't usually drink so much especially out in public. I looked in the dining room, the drawing room, the main foyer and the living room, no Michael. Why couldn't I find him? The house was big, but not that darn big. Finally I spotted him in the library talking to Madeline's husband Judge Enrique Kennedy, and some other judges and councilmen. Michael's firm did all of their accounting so wining and dining with business contacts was not only good business, but necessary business. For Jackie to behave like this in front of all these people was disturbing; it could affect Michael's business and she knew that. If it weren't for knowing I had the best relationship with my husband over anyone in the world, I would put Jackie and Michael right up there with us. I walked up to the group of men.

"Excuse me gentleman, but I need to speak to Michael for a moment please."

"Evelyn, it's good to see you. And where is that husband of yours?" Enrique asked me.

"Oh you know Tony; he's around here somewhere. I saw him earlier talking with your wife. She was probably trying to talk him into breaking our plans to make the gala next month."

"Oh that woman, you know how she is." He laughed.

"Yes, I do."

"Michael, can you come with me for a moment please?" I pulled Michael to a quiet spot in the room.

"Hey Ev, what's up?"

"You tell me! What's going on with Jackie?" I asked him. He looked at me strangely.

"Nothing! Why?" He replied.

"Why? Why?" I blustered, just flabbergasted. "She is drunk off her ass that's why." He gaped at me, open mouthed like a fish. I'm glad he was an accountant he would have made a lousy attorney being stuck for words like this.

"What do you mean she's drunk?" He said sounding so perplexed I almost felt sorry for him.

"Like I said, drunk off her ass, though she can still walk. Her speech is slurred, and if I turn my head for even a moment she gets another drink." A stricken and panicked look came over his face as he turned as if searching for Jackie in the room. "Don't worry," I said trying to calm him. "Ava is with her and won't let her drink anymore." I could see the instant relief wash over his face.

"Well we'll go home. I'll just tell everyone that she is sick."

"No, no don't do that she knows it's important for you to be here and she wants to stay but you just need to be on alert." I wanted so much to ask him was there something going on with him and Jackie but I just couldn't ask that. Well, I could, but I needed to ask Jackie when she was sober. My sister was not acting like my sister.

"Okay, I'll just go and be with her," he said. "Dinner should be ready soon and as soon as it's over I can take her home."

"Good, she's in the living room over by the buffet table." I told him and he quickly turned and went to retrieve his wife. I could not wait until this night was over.

* * * *

We finally made it home near eleven o'clock that night. My feet were hurting, and my eyes were tired. I was just plain exhausted. Walking into our bedroom, I didn't think I had the energy to undress and take off my make-up. "Tony, from here on out, no more dinners, galas, nothing;" I said as I huffed my way into the dressing closet.

"You say that every time we come home past ten."

"And I mean it each and every time, but I always let you talk me out of it," I called out from the closet.

"You love me honey, you can't help it." He said teasing me.

"Yeah, you're my kryptonite," I said flippantly back. I could hear him laughing at me in his closet. I finally got undressed and into my pj's. Now I needed to take off my make-up. Uggh, thank God for the makers of Oil of Olay to make it quick and easy, but I still didn't want to do it.

"Evelyn!" I heard Tony call to me.

"Yeah!"

"What was wrong with Jackie?"

"You mean you couldn't tell? She was drunk!"

"What!!" He said shocked, choking on his toothpaste.

"Yes. She was drunk, walking crooked, and slurring her speech. Michael told her not to talk, and he told everyone that she wasn't feeling that well, but she didn't want to go home." That part was true anyway.

"Jackie has never done anything like that before. Has she?"

"Not that I'm aware so maybe it was just like she said. She just got to drinking and before you know it she was sloshed. And she was drinking on an empty stomach, so she probably did get drunk really fast." The more I thought about it the more it made sense.

"Well, that's seems to be a reasonable explanation, don't put anymore thought into it." He told me.

"Yeah you're right. Good night." I turned to kiss him as we got into bed. He put his arm around me like always.

Chapter Six

The next morning I couldn't wait to talk to Jackie, despite her words of only drinking on an empty stomach. I decided to make my morning run to her house, which is normally not the way I go but I knew I couldn't wait until later in the day. Being the early riser that she is I knew she would be awake. Making my run to her house caused me to have to run a few extra miles uphill and though I felt like my lungs were on fire I pushed on to the prize of her back kitchen door. As I ran up her driveway she was standing at the door seemingly waiting for me.

"Good morning Evelyn, I knew you would be coming!" She said to me as she turned back into the house but kept the back door open, waiting for me.

"Whew!" I said out of breath, plunking myself down at her kitchen table in front of a glass of water she had just set down. "How?" I said while trying to catch my breath. "did you?" I continued to try and talk, still catching my breath, "know I would be here this morning?" I finally got out the rest of my sentence.

"Ev, first drink your water. And what do you mean, how did I know?" She challenged my question. "I thought we grew up together. I know exactly what each of my sisters will do depending on the circumstance, and since you run in the mornings I knew you would run yourself over here and then I will have to drive you home." She said haughtily! She was right of course.

"Well Ms. Jackie you don't have to sound so smug now, do you?"

"Of course I do, when you try to pretend we both didn't know you were coming over this morning. Anyway, Ava already called and I will tell you the same thing I told her, nothing is wrong. I just got carried away drinking on an empty stomach. I'm actually embarrassed." I didn't believe that for a minute. First off she was in too good a mood, the entire time she tried to tell me off, she's had a smile on her face.

"Unh huh!" I said to her suspiciously. "Why don't I believe you?"

"You don't believe me because you're an evil person."

"Well perhaps this evil person would believe you if you didn't have that little smile on your face."

"Okay, I'm not embarrassed. I would be if I had actually done something and made a fool of myself, but since I didn't I'm not, and it was an accident."

"Well, what did Michael say?" I asked.

"He thought something was wrong with me as well. I understand considering he's known me almost as long as you have and I've never done that before. If I had done anything to hurt his career I don't know what I would have said to him and then I would have had to face Daddy and that would have been even worse, but since I didn't and it was an accident, I will be much more careful in the future."

"Well, I'm glad to hear it." I told her as I gave her a hug. "Now drive me home." And we burst out laughing.

When I got back home I was rushing to get ready for work since I had detoured to Jackie's house that morning. Normally I would have believed my sister's excuse, and she almost had me until I was leaving. I offered to take the trash out and saw quite a few empty liquor bottles in her recycle bin next to the cans. I didn't know what to say and I didn't have time so I pretended that I hadn't seen anything amiss and just let her drive me home, but this was not the end of this by a long shot.

In the kitchen I told Janice what happened with Jackie, her perfectly believable explanation until I saw the liquor bottles in her recycle bins.

"Well, you don't see her everyday so possibly she and Michael have been having some parties over there or something." Janice said trying to come up with a plausible explanation.

"Jackie does not have parties and not invite me!"

"Yeah, I guess you're right about that. She doesn't usually do anything without you unless it's with Michael. So I suppose you're right that something is going on with her." Janice exclaimed.

"She's never kept things from me before and now she's drinking! I don't like this at all and I'm feeling betrayed. We've never kept secrets and now we're in our forties and she starts keeping them. Gwen keeps secrets, Adele keeps secrets, but never Ava or Jackie, at least not from me. I should've just confronted her then and there. I'm going back over there right now." I was practically shouting now having worked myself into a state.

"No you will not, Evelyn. You just calm yourself down right now. You and Jackie have the closest relationship of sisters I have ever seen, and her keeping you out is hurting your feelings. I understand that, but don't let hurt feelings cause problems between you and her. If she's keeping something from you, then trust that it must be something important to her and she wouldn't do anything to hurt you." Janice hugged me as she talked to me soothingly to calm me down. By this time I was crying silent tears because it wasn't just that Jackie was keeping things from me but it had to be something she felt was bad to keep from me, and it hurt that she didn't come to me to share that hurt or to see if I could help her.

"I just want to know what is causing her to drink or if Michael is drinking then him. We're not some young kids!" I cried.

"I know." Janice continued to soothe. "Just give her time. Perhaps on your trip in a few weeks she will be more forthcoming when you all are in a relaxed and fun atmosphere."

"I hope so. But by then even if she's not," I said as I pulled away from Janice and was wiping my face, "I will confront her on this and demand to know what in hell is going on." After that I ran back upstairs to fix my make-up.

Chapter Seven

We had finally arrived at the day of our trip and it was an ice cold morning. Jackie, Ava and Gwen arrived together and had just come into the kitchen where Janice and I were talking while she was making us a huge breakfast of sausage, bacon, grits, eggs, gravy and hash browns as well as her wonderful coffee.

"Good morning ladies!" I said in greeting. They each greeted me in return.

"Everybody sit down so you can eat. I'm cooking breakfast for you all." Janice instructed us.

"You don't have to tell me twice. I'm starving." Ava hurriedly sat down eagerly waiting to be fed.

"Ooh! Me too, I'm starving." Gwen seconded. As we all sat and began eating, everyone else strolled in one behind the other. I couldn't believe Adele wasn't just on time but was early, decked out to the nines as always, but if she weren't I would have assumed that there was a zombie in her place. My kitchen was huge so we could all sit at the table or at my oversized island; we all chose to sit around the table.

"What happened to the van we were supposed to have rented? I don't see it!" Adele asked.

"To be honest they were ugly so I had Alicia rent us two Cadillac Escalades SUV's instead. They were delivered yesterday and are parked in the back in front of the garage. I didn't want them blocking places for you to park your cars on the street." I told them. They chorused that having the Escalades were much better than the vans. "But I'm still not driving!" I stated.

"Evelyn you're still afraid to drive in Tennessee?" Adele asked. They all turned to look at me.

"I'm not afraid to drive in Tennessee." I told them. "I'm afraid to drive on the highway in Tennessee. It's too curvy and I feel like we could just drive right off the mountainside and fall to our deaths." They all had the nerve to laugh at me before they went back to their own discussions but I was serious. I didn't care; I just knew I wasn't driving and that's all that mattered.

"I don't know if everyone plans to actually ski or take the skiing lessons but I bought everyone helmets. I didn't know what the color of your outerwear was going to be, so I just got black for everyone," I told them. "No one is going to die like that movie star did." Everyone was very pleased and grateful for thinking of their safety when it never crossed their minds and offered to pay me back for the purchases. "I don't want any money; it was a gift." I told them. And I would never have put that type of financial pressure on Anne. I thought to myself.

"Janice, why aren't you coming with us?" Gwen asked her.

"John and I already have a vacation planned and I didn't want to spend any extra money." I loved Janice; all my family could afford this trip easily, but if they couldn't they would never hint that they didn't have enough money to do anything. But Janice didn't care what anyone thought, she was just an open person. You gotta love people like that!

"Okay everyone," I said, interrupting the multiple conversations going on. "I didn't want any strange attitudes so I decided we would draw for SUV one or SUV two and that is what we stick to."

"Evelyn, why must you treat us like children?" Adele complained.

"Because past experiences have taught me that no matter how old we become it's very easy to mimic children!" Adele rolled her eyes at me. I just smiled at her in return. Everyone else laughed! Ok, here's the cup, obviously there are four number one's and four number two's. Adele, we'll start with you, just take one and pass it on but call out your number when you pull it." I handed her the cup. She reached in and grabbed a slip of paper with some weird flourish of the hand. I loved my sister but boy was she a drama queen, but I suppose out of five girls we were bound to have at least one. She was a lot like my mother.

"One," Adele called out as she passed the cup to Gwen.

"Two," said Gwen.

"Two," said Jackie.

"One," said Katherine.

"One," said Ava.

"Two," said Sheila.

"Two," said Anne and that left me with a one.

"Okay, everyone has their numbers. Ava, will you drive down there?"

"Yes, that's fine," she answered.

"Who will drive down in the second one?" I asked.

"I will," Sheila volunteered.

"Well, if everyone is finished eating, let's get all our stuff and get this show on the road."

After packing the SUVS with all of the luggage, programming the GPS devices, and Janice hugging us all goodbye and wishing us a safe journey, we prayed and hit the road. We were making good time until we hit the Tennessee border and the weather changed from cold and clear to frigid and lots of snow. This was also why I chose to sit in the backseat, it was easier to close my eyes and pretend that I couldn't imagine us driving off the mountain side plummeting into hell.

We finally made it not in five hours as planned, but in eight because the weather went from scary to horrific, but Ava wasn't afraid of anything and she handled that big thing as if she did it every day. Apparently Sheila held up just fine as well. Jackie called us from the other SUV to see how we were doing while we were on the road. I seemed to be the only one that was ready to have a heart attack at any moment. Where did they get all those brave genes from or why didn't I get them while God was handing them out?!I felt like kissing the ground but I didn't want to embarrass myself. We did manage to stop at a little mart to grab some groceries to have something for the evening to cook and eat before we headed up the mountain to the chalet office to pick up the keys in the lockbox. Driving up the mountain road to the chalet was also a terrorizing event. It was pitch black and you could drive off the mountain if you missed a turn in the blackness. And there are bears out here somewhere. Of course we didn't see any, but they advise to make it back up the mountain before it gets dark each day because you can't see. That was the plan but the weather had changed all that. What made me come up with Pigeon Forge Tennessee in the middle of the winter to go to? I'm a glutton for punishment!

"Everyone," I heard Jackie shouting at us all, "let's hurry up and get this stuff and get in the chalet before a bear comes and eats us." No one had to be told twice. We all kicked into bionic women mode. We all dropped our bags as soon as we got in the door.

"I'm so tired!" Ava exclaimed as she went and sat on the living room couch. And I'm sure she was after all that strenuous driving in such bad weather.

"I am too!" Sheila said as she collapsed on the couch beside her.

"We're all tired, but of course you two will be exhausted. You drove the entire way and in this horrid weather." Jackie added. We had all collapsed by this time upon various furniture pieces around the room.

"Come on everybody if we sit here too long we won't get up again. Let's find a bedroom and as soon as I can get a shower, I will start on dinner," Sheila said. Everyone agreed as we slowly got up, grabbing bags. I felt like I was going to drop. I was still stressed from the fear of the ride. A shower sounded wonderful, but I first had to call Tony.

* * * *

"Hello," I said as he answered the call.

"Why are you just now calling?"

"We just got here. The weather got really bad as soon as we crossed into Tennessee. Then we had to go up the mountain like a turtle since you know it's pitch black up here, and we didn't want to fall to our deaths." I said agitated from my stressed state.

"Are you sure you're all right?" I could hear his worry for me through the phone.

"I'm a bit shaky still. But I'm going to take a shower then help cook dinner. We picked up some wine, so that should help as well.

By the time I'm ready for bed I should have all my kinks worked out."

"If none of that helps, you better call me back." He said in a soothing tone.

"I will." I promised him. He was my rock and the most wonderful man in the world.

"All right. Go take your shower. I love you."

"I love you too." I said just before disconnecting.

Chapter Eight

Everyone seemed to get a second wind after taking a shower, as we congregated in the kitchen preparing dinner, someone hooked up her IPod to the stereo system that was provided by the chalet and we all started dancing and singing and drinking. It felt like I was twenty-two again and glancing around the room at all my loved ones in the room, I'm sure they were feeling just as young and light as I felt. Sheila was cooking her famous (only to us), but delicious- (definitely true), stir fry chicken and sausage. It was filled with tons of vegetables and rice and spicy seasonings. It was definitely a family favorite! We helped her by cutting up all the ingredients.

After dinner we decided to play Monopoly, a game I never seemed to have any luck at, and it didn't seem like I was going to break my streak tonight.

"I'm on a roll tonight!" Sheila yelled out gleefully as she bankrupted Jackie and put her out of the game. From the money on the table, it seemed Gwen was going to be her next victim for bankruptcy as soon as she had her turn and landed on Sheila's true monopoly of the board.

"Oh shut up!" We all yelled back laughing.

"You're just a bunch of sore losers; take your turn so I can take your money." Sheila was really rubbing it into us tonight. It must be all those glasses of wine she drank, we all drank actually. I think we finished three bottles already. Thank goodness we didn't plan anything for our first full day except for real grocery shopping for the week. None of us would make anything scheduled in our varied degrees of drunkenness. If we were anywhere else where people could see us we'd be embarrassing ourselves. Being from such an influential family we always had to maintain a perfect image or it would be on the news or in the newspaper or even Facebook. It could get exhausting being recognized all the time, so being somewhere people don't have a clue who you are or could not care less was refreshing. However, thinking about our image drew my attention to Jackie at the far end of the table, who lately wasn't holding up her seventh of the Isaacs offspring good behavior in public responsibility.

"Hey Jackie!" I called out. I cleared my throat not exactly sure how to approach the subject. Being very tipsy, there was no way I could hold it in any longer, especially after what I discovered since we had arrived earlier in the evening. "Well!" I continued. "I went into your room while you were in the shower because I forgot my facial loofah at home and I know you use the same kind and knew you always bring extra."

"Oh really!" She said. "That's no problem. You know I don't care. You didn't even have to tell me."

"Yeah I know, but…." I wasn't sure how I wanted to say this. I knew I was stalling. "Remember when we were at the Kennedys' dinner party and you were drunk?" All of a sudden the entire room was quiet; it went from everyone talking loud a mile a minute to utter silence in a heartbeat.

"Drunk?" Adele asked Jackie in shock. "You were drunk?" Adele asked her again. Everyone was staring at Jackie asking the same question just only with their eyes. Jackie was staring at me.

"Yeah. Of course I remember. But it was only one time, so no big deal. You agreed and laughed it off with me." She said, defending herself, sounding offended and embarrassed, but trying not to show it.

"And I still agree because nothing happened to out you being drunk. The reason I brought it up is because when I went to find the loofah, I went into your closet and I didn't know which suitcase to look in, while I was reaching for one, my arm knocked into another one and it started clinking. This worried me because I didn't say anything but I remembered seeing all those empty liquor bottles in your trash so I looked in your suitcase. I saw multiple bottles of gin, bourbon and scotch in your suitcase." I realized I had been talking really fast and my words had all run together. I had forgotten to take a breath so I finally exhaled. All of a sudden Adele, Gwen, Katherine and Anne were bombarding her with questions and telling her she needed AA. I rolled my eyes; we had no clue if her drinking was truly out of control or anything but of course she needed AA. Ava said nothing, I assume because she was there at the drunken occasion and was being patient to see what Jackie would say. Sheila said nothing but she rarely gave her opinion unless it was asked. She was great for consoling people though!

As the music played, Adele droned on about what if she would have done something to embarrass the firm, mama and daddy. Gwen said she might embarrass everyone else and on and on. And still the music played on and Jackie stuck her tongue out at me. Yes, my sister was forty-six years old and I was forty-eight and I had grandchildren but I stuck my tongue right back at her. In some ways you just never grow up especially when it's you and your family. She started looking a little sad. I realized I started a train wreck situation but I also realized I was more than tipsy so I didn't care.

"I'm not an alcoholic, people!" Jackie said angrily as she scowled at us and gave me an extra scowl.

"Okay, so why are you now traveling with suitcases full of liquor as well as having recycle bins full of even more bottles?" I asked her. All of a sudden she burst in tears, I mean body-racking sobs. Sheila, Lord love her, was on the job immediately running around the table wrapping her in her arms, while I was still in shock of the sudden change of rebellious sticking out tongue to an emotional wreck. Apparently we were all in shock because it took the rest of us about thirty seconds to catch up to Jackie's rocket speed emotional shift. We all hugged Jackie in turn, I would have held her longer, but Sheila was on the job and she wouldn't let me.

"So," Sheila said to her soothingly for probably the twentieth time. "What is wrong? We know it's not just us asking you questions, so it has to be something else." Jackie was still crying her eyes out. She managed to slow the crying down but was still gulping large sobs until she screeched out what none of us ever expected to hear right before laying her head on Sheila's shoulder and crying full blast again.

"Michael is having an affair!"

Chapter Nine

We had all been struck mute; if the great Marvin Gaye wasn't playing on the stereo I'm sure you could have heard a pin drop. As my sister, not just my sister but one of my favorite sisters sat in misery, I felt a strange sensation building inside me, a very unwanted sensation, I knew I had to get out of there. I turned and practically flew out the room; I took the stairs two and three at a time barely hearing Ava and I think Katherine calling after me. I would have made my daughter Alex proud at my speed of conquering the steps. As I sprinted through the house that feeling was about to burst from me. I ran into my room and slammed the door, ran into my bathroom and slammed the door, grabbed a thick towel, smashed it over my face, and commenced to laugh my butt off.

I was laughing so hard I couldn't breathe, and my stomach was in extreme pain because I couldn't get any air from laughing so hard. I felt horrible for laughing at Jackie when she was in such misery, and I wasn't really laughing at her but the situation was just hilarious because it was so ridiculous. Just as I thought I was beginning to get a hold of myself, Ava knocked on the bathroom door.

"Evelyn? Are you okay?"

"Yes, I'm fine." I was barely able to conceal my laugh that had also turned into tears, so I kept the towel pushed into my face to muffle me. "Tell everyone that I'm fine and I will be there in a few minutes to see about Jackie."

"Sure, but what about you? Seeing you so upset over Jackie's marriage has me worried about you." I had to get her out of here before I gave my real condition away.

"Ava honey, I'll be fine. Please just go back and help take care of Jackie and I will be down soon. Can you do that for me?"

"Are you sure?"

"I promise you I'm sure. I'll be down in just a little while." I heard Ava walk away and close my bedroom door. I started thinking about what Jackie said and again I lost the battle to stop laughing. I felt terrible. I was being a very terrible person laughing at her misery, but that wasn't it. Michael is the nicest, sweetest, kindest man you could ever meet, and he worships the air Jackie breathes. But that wasn't the kicker, Michael is a NERD. She brought him home to meet us for the first time when she was nineteen. None of us could figure out what she saw in him. He was very tall, kind of cute in looks, extremely smart, but he was the biggest nerd we had ever seen; you could just picture him as a child and in that vision you saw a nerd baby. We didn't know what to think except nerd or geeky nerd until we saw how in love and devoted he was to Jackie and how he doted on her and then we all understood what Jackie saw in him or rather we tried! They have been married for twenty-five years, and in all those years he has never looked at her with any less love and devotion that he has always looked at her. There was no way Michael was cheating on Jackie; my sister is losing her mind. I had to get my emotions under control before I allowed myself back downstairs. I wonder was my sister smoking something that brought hallucinations or paranoia on, because this made no sense to me. My sister has lost her mind, I just know it. Now we would have a crazy one in the bunch. Daddy with his perfect Isaacs children would be no more. That thought brought my laughing fit back in full force. We are so not perfect, only jealous idiots had proclaimed that our family said we were of course, being a black prominent family, coming from wealth, high education and influence, everyone believed we said that about ourselves, so that when we fell from grace, they could say we had it coming. I needed to get myself together to find out exactly why Jackie thought this of Michael. After a few more minutes finally getting myself calm, I washed my face for the full effect to show I had been crying from sorrow and not laughter. I headed back downstairs where I could now hear Rick James on the stereo. A very nice variety of music was playing. Everyone was still sitting at the kitchen table where I had left them; I walked over to Jackie. As she saw me approaching her, she stood up and turned to me. I raised my arms and she ran into them.

"I'm sorry I ran upstairs but I was so upset;" I lied, "that I didn't want my feelings affecting you more." That was true.

"It's all right," she said. She was still crying but it had wound down to just sniffles by this time.

"Jackie, why do you think Michael is having an affair?" I asked her this as I directed her to sit back down. I looked around the table at everyone and I could tell they thought Jackie was losing it as well. This was our Jackie whom we loved more than anything, but we just couldn't believe this of Michael, not without stone hard proof. Jackie still hadn't answered me, so I turned to look at the others.

"What did I miss?" I asked.

"Nothing. She hasn't said anything else to us." Gwen said.

"Jackie, please tell us why you're saying and feel this way." I begged her.

"You won't believe me." Jackie said in barely a whisper.

"What do you mean we won't believe you? Do you think we would call you a liar?" Adele demanded, very much offended by the thought.

"Adele!" I snapped. "This is not about you, or us." I had to admit to myself I agreed with Adele on being offended but now was not the time. Ava moved her chair close to Jackie and took her hand to talk to her.

"We know you are not a liar and would never call you that. We are your family and we love you. We just want to know details so we can try and help you." Ava pleaded with her in a comforting tone while massaging her hands.

"Well," Jackie finally began to talk and we all seemed to take a collective breath.

"Michael hired a new personal assistant a few months ago named Yolanda. I met her right after she started, when I came into the office to pick Michael up for our weekly lunch date. She's around forty and very pretty. She seemed nice enough, but I didn't like her." Jackie reached for her glass and took a sip of her drink and just sat there. We waited thinking she would automatically begin again but that didn't happen. We waited and we waited. She just sat there as if what she said, said it all, but she'd said nothing.

"Well?!!!" We all finally said. We couldn't have done any better if we rehearsed it. She actually jumped as if we shocked her.

"Jackie, you have got to do better than that." Adele screamed. "This Yolanda person being pretty and you not liking her is not enough to, to, to well, not enough for anything." Adele was about to blow a gasket.

"She acted nice, but I could tell it was like she didn't want me there. I felt like she was sizing me up." Jackie finally continued.

"Excuse me, but Michael is your husband and it's his firm." Gwen said, already mad in Jackie's defense, though we still had heard nothing at this point. Honestly I knew my sisters and myself and as soon as Jackie mentioned the name Yolanda we mentally had put her head on the chopping block, so she was guilty in our eyes. But, we were raised by a judge, which meant we had to hear the evidence and at least pretend we were open-minded. We still had heard nothing. Jackie finally started talking and it was like a switch had been turned up because now she was talking nonstop.

"Well, like I said, I felt it when I first met her when I came to meet Michael for our weekly lunch date, but I ignored it, thinking it was me. You know I sometimes just stop in to see him if I'm downtown shopping or something, and then I may stay awhile and visit with my son or Benjamin." Jackie's son was also named Michael and he was an associate attorney at the firm and Benjamin was my son-in-law, an accountant who worked for Michael. Jackie continued. "The more I stopped in, the more I noticed how she would look at me and how her dress was changing. At first she was dressed really professionally, but then she started dressing very sexy and provocative-like in really low-cut blouses and tight short skirts and dresses. And I still ignored her because I've never interfered with who works for Michael or in his business in general. Then Michael started working late and when I would call to see when he would be home, she would answer or he would just say he would be home soon. Michael doesn't usually work late, but all of a sudden he hires her and now he's working late a few nights a week." Jackie was now crying again.

"Jackie honey," Gwen pressed. "Did you ask Michael why he was working late?"

"Noooo, I couldn't." She was now gulping sobs again. We all sat looking at her and then at each other.

"Jackie," I said. "It will be alright, we will make it alright; I promise." Everyone agreed in unison.

"But how can it be alright when I'm losing my husband to Yolanda big boobs?" I wanted to laugh but I was able to stave it off this time. I leaned in close to Jackie and held her face in both my hands and kissed her. I glanced a look around at the rest of my sisters for a quick confirmation of their nods. "Jackie, I just promised you that it would be alright. That's all you need to know. Now go to bed, you're drunk!" As Anne helped Jackie out of the room and up the stairs to her room so she wouldn't break her neck, I remembered the sadness on her beautiful face and all I could do was think. Yolanda was going down!

Chapter Ten

The next morning we were moving slower than normal, which was expected with all the drinking we did. Since we would be here nearly a week, I decided to take my chances on the treadmill in the in- house workout room for my morning run, definitely feeling I might fall off in my hangover state. Thank goodness there was more than one treadmill since Ava was already in a full run on one when I walked in. I nodded good morning to her, turned on my IPod and set my run for five hill miles. I would love to do a straight flat run, but Cincinnati was anything but flat, so I would just be setting myself up for extreme exhaustion when I got back and hit the pavement. As I started to hit my stride and ease into my run, I began to relax and feel good and think about our upcoming week of events. Even after all the drama of last night I was more than looking forward to this trip. I noticed Gwen and Adele had come in but at this point I couldn't break my concentration and speak to them, still afraid I would slip and fall. We all ran; my dad had made us growing up and it had stuck for the most part. Gwen and I were the only ones who ran marathons, but everyone ran a few miles a day. Gwen took Ava's place on the treadmill when she finished and Adele got on the elliptical machine. As I looked at Adele I wondered why I hadn't gotten on the elliptical instead or even bought one for home; that would fit me so much better. I'd have to think more about that when we returned home.

When I came into the kitchen after my run and shower, everyone seemed to already be there including Jackie who I hadn't expected to be up until much later.

"Evelyn, we were just making the grocery list. Take a look and see if there is anything we are missing or you may want." Sheila said while handing me the list and a plate of pancakes as I sat down to eat.

"Uh, sure and thanks for the pancakes." I hated to have to think before I had a chance to eat or drink coffee, including a simple grocery list. I just wasn't wired for anything before I ate, so I pretended to study the list as I ate. I loved Sheila, and my brother Harper could not have been blessed with a better wife, but she had way too much energy. I swear she never seemed to stop moving or get tired, and she was extremely organized. If you were running for some type of office she was great to run your campaign or anything for that matter. She was a bit bossy as well!

"How are you feeling this morning Jackie?" I asked her while continuing to stuff my face. I was starving for some reason.

"I'm pretty good. I'm really sorry about last night. I'm so embarrassed." Jackie had lowered her head while she spoke.

"Hey, pick your head up." I told her. "You were raised better; there is no reason to be embarrassed especially in front of us. Just try to put it out of your mind this week so you can have a good time. We'll deal with everything else when we get home." We shared a smile between us; we had a special bond that neither of us shared with our other sisters. Ava was our baby but Jackie and I were always like a tag team; though I wanted to slap her for not sharing her worries with me before she'd practically turned into a drunk over it. I'd have to wait until it was all over before I shared my feelings on that subject with her. I could prioritize if nothing else.

I finally looked over the grocery list once my tummy was nice and full and it looked fine to me except there was no candy on the list and I love candy. I added chocolate and licorice, my favorites.

"Sheila, I added some candy but other than that the list looks fine to me. Who's going to the store with you?" I already knew Sheila was going.

"Adele and Ava said they were coming with me." Sheila answered. "We'll be going soon so we can get it out of the way. After we get back and get the food put away, I thought we could all go down into Gatlinburg and shop or whatever. What do you think?" Why did she always refer to me like I was the leader of the pack?!! But I just answered her.

"That sounds good to me as long as everyone else wants to go. I'll be ready when you get back." When they left for the grocery store the rest of us cleaned up the kitchen and then dressed so we would be ready to go after we put the groceries away. I was sitting on the couch relaxing looking out the window at the beautiful Smoky Mountains when I saw the SUV coming up the drive. They had returned!

"Everybody, they're back," I called through the house. We all grabbed our coats and headed outside to get the groceries.

After putting away all the groceries, we were back in the trucks heading down the mountain. I sat myself right in the backseat once more. As my stomach dipped, I closed my eyes and prayed and thought again. What had caused me to lose my mind and choose a destination on a mountain? But there was nothing but to deal with it now; I was here and my money was spent.

We ended up having a really good time shopping, taking in all the sites and attractions with the most fun being The Wonder Works Museum. I was reminded of when we were teenagers, when only school and having fun were all we thought about. We decided to eat at a local steak house instead of going back to cook that evening, and everyone was in good spirits. The waiter had just taken our order when Katherine asked about skiing the next day.

"Evelyn, how are you supposed to take lessons if you're afraid to be on the mountain?"

"I'm not afraid of being on the mountain I'm afraid of driving off the mountain. It's a difference. I can't explain it, but it just feels like we will just drive off the side and plummet to our deaths." They all actually laughed at me. I glared back at them for making fun of me, though if I had to admit it and only to myself. If it weren't me they were laughing at, I would be laughing with them.

"Enough with picking on me." I had to change the subject. "Is everyone taking the lessons tomorrow? It's all paid for!"

"Oh yes, I'm looking forward to it," Anne said excitedly.

"I just hope I don't break anything, I'm too old to start breaking bones," Adele added and we all laughed. Our food came and we all dug in heartedly.

"This is really good, I was worried it wouldn't be very good. They aren't known for fine cuisine around here." Gwen was a bit of a food snob so it wasn't surprising to hear that comment from her. What was surprising was that Adele didn't chime in with agreement since she was the bigger snob but as I looked down the table she was too busy concentrating on her plate but then she looked up with a mouth full and mumbled, "hmm mmm." Everyone was happy!

* * * *

The next day found us at the ski lodge filled with partly concealed fear mixed with excitement waiting for our first skiing lesson to begin. Noticing that Adele stood out in particular from the rest of us I walked over to her.

"Adele, we are about to fall on our butts trying to ski. Why are you wearing so much jewelry?" She had on three gold chains, a pair of diamond and hoop earrings, bracelets and three to four fingers on each hand had rings on them.

"What do you mean?! This is about what I always wear."

"Yes I know, but most days you are not standing on top of a ski slope about to learn to ski."

"I can't just not be me Evelyn, skiing or not!" I just shook my head and rolled my eyes. My mother always told me to stop rolling my eyes or they would get stuck; I was beginning to believe her. My eye hurt with that roll.

We were on the bunny slopes for our lessons but I have to tell you, being over forty and falling was a bit scary, but also very fun. I managed to ski about fifteen feet before falling after two hours of lessons! Thank goodness I stayed in shape, because I knew I was still going to be sore; it would be double if I didn't. We all managed to learn to walk on the skis as instructed, except for Katherine who went toppling over head-first every time. Thank God for the helmets I thought, and that she wasn't a baby because I would be worried about her soft spot if she still had one. It was hilarious!

After we had a snack, Anne, Jackie and Ava decided to stay and practice on their own on the baby slopes while the rest of us went back to the chalet. We gave Katherine two extra strength pain meds and put her to bed. We realized we could all use a nap so we decided to hit the sack as well.

I was awakened suddenly but didn't understand why, then awareness hit me all at once. There was yelling coming from inside the house. What in the world was going on? I leapt from the bed and ran towards the yelling. The voices were coming from the living room I realized running down the stairs. When I got there Adele, Jackie, Ava, Gwen and Sheila were yelling at each other. Anne was crying and I immediately felt dejavu from yesterday when Jackie was the one crying. Katherine was gulping back more pain meds. We were on vacation; what was all this crying and arguing about? Again!!!

"What is going on?" I yelled, but no one was listening. They just kept on yelling and screaming at each other. Then something happened that I thought could never possibly happen in my lifetime. Adele pulled back her arm and slapped Jackie with so much force that Jackie nearly fell over. For a moment the room was dead silent. I was in shock as I was sure everyone else was as well. All of a sudden, all hell broke loose. Jackie reached and slapped her in return just as hard and Adele seemed to be shocked that she was hit back. Then Jackie tackled Adele and commenced to start punching her. They were rolling around fighting. Fist-were flying. I couldn't believe this, not my sisters. Gwen and Ava were trying to pull them apart when Gwen got taken down in the middle. She dropped like a sack of bricks. It was like when George Foremen knocked out Joe Frazier. Yelling, "Down goes Frazier" would have been inappropriate, especially since now I was crying. I didn't exactly know how to help stop it without getting punched or slapped myself. But I was crying because my beautiful, crazy sisters who were raised never to raise a hand against one another in anger, had obviously lost their minds and were actually fighting like hooligans in the street. And they were middle-aged grown women. Adele and Jackie were fifty-one and forty-six respectively, and Adele was a grandmother like me, which also made her fighting like this even more ridiculous. After about ten minutes they seemed to start running out of steam and suddenly stopped and sat up with their legs sprawled out in front of them breathing hard. This time I screamed at the top of my lungs.

"What in the hell is going on?!!!!"

Chapter Eleven

They were all just staring at me as if I had spoken a foreign language they didn't speak.

"Did I not get woken up out of my sleep with screaming and yelling, and then come in to see one of you slap the other and then all hell break loose?" I was so angry and confused I could barely talk. "And now no one wants to say anything?" I continued screaming. "Daddy would be so hurt and ashamed at what just happened. Have you lost your minds? And we are middle age for Christ sake!" I said disgusted. They were all just staring at one another. Then Gwen spoke up. She was holding her face, obviously having gotten hit hard when Jackie and Adele took her down.

"Apparently when we all came back here and they stayed up at the resort to ski some more, at some point while they were there, Anne saw her husband there with another woman."

"What?!!!" I screamed as I whipped my head to look at Anne. I couldn't believe what I had just heard; this just didn't seem to be possible. Anne had tears streaming down her face as she cried silently.

"Do you mean," I continued, "to tell me that he knew we would be here and he came anyway to do this on purpose?" I wasn't really asking anyone in particular, I couldn't wrap this type of emotional cruelty around my mind or the situation in general. This wasn't making any sense.

"No," Anne began talking softly. "We haven't been getting along well for a while now and when I told him I wanted to go on this trip with you all, he just said go but don't ask him for any money and to leave him alone. That's why Jackie gave me the money so I could come." She looked away as she said this; I could see the shame in her eyes and also hear it in her voice. I couldn't deal with feelings right now. I put this on the list for later.

"Okay, so how did we get from seeing Anne's husband to Adele and Jackie fighting like animals?"

"Jackie." This time it was Adele who spoke up and she was still so mad she was practically frothing at the mouth. "Jackie decided that she would interfere. She somehow found out what cabin they were staying in, stole the key from housekeeping, broke in and cut up all their clothes, poured bleach on their clothes then found his car and poured bleach in his gas tank. But somehow, she managed to leave the bleach container with her fingerprints on it in the freaking cabin." As Adele was spewing this out with venom in her voice, I had closed my eyes in pain picturing the scene in my head.

"Oh Jackie, what possessed you to do that?" I asked her as my vision became cloudy and my head began to swim.

"I saw him and in my mind it was Michael and that Yolanda and I just had to do something." I squeezed my eyes shut tight.

"Yeah, but why were you two fighting? This still does not explain that."

"She went into the security office and somehow looked on their computer and found the information and then she went into housekeeping and stole the key off the housekeeping cart. In front of the cameras!" Adele whaled in outrage!

At this point I thought I was going to pass out, I felt my legs getting weak as I slumped onto the couch. I put my head between my legs as I began to hyperventilate. Oh God I thought. What were we going to do? Oh Mama and Daddy, they were old, this would surely put them in their graves when we were all arrested. Jackie, for the actual crime; the rest of us for aiding and abetting. And it looked as if we planned the crime. No one would believe we ran into him accidentally. If I hadn't planned the trip I wouldn't believe it either, but I don't know her husband from Adam's house cat.

Jackie began crying and apologizing. "I'm sorry, I wasn't thinking." Adele was having none of it, apparently everyone was upset about what Jackie did but not to the level that Adele let herself go. Adele was screaming and getting madder instead of calmer; her face had gotten dark red with anger and she had her fist balled up so tight I'm sure she was hurting herself with her nails.

"We are the Isaacs, not some Johnsons or Browns or anyone else but the Isaacs," Adele shouted at Jackie. Oh God I thought, here she goes on her we're the Isaacs rant.

"We are the most prominent and influential black family in southern Ohio and the tri states." I wasn't sure that was true but definitely Cincinnati and Northern Kentucky, but I didn't refute her. Even if I wanted to, I wouldn't have been able to; I don't think my mouth was working in coordination with my brain. "We have a reputation to uphold," Adele continued screaming on. "Our daddy is a retired judge, our brother is a judge, and our other brother is the freaking mayor. I'm an attorney, my husband is an attorney, and Gwen and her husband are attorneys. Ava and her husband are attorneys, Evelyn is married to an attorney; we have children who are attorneys. Our firm is our name and we are the best. We have businesses in multiple states. How dare you risk it all with this stunt?"

A family full of lawyers, we had to sound like the most boring stiff shirt family in the history of boring stiff shirt families. But we actually knew how to have fun and cut a rug like they use to say just like any other family when we weren't in the public eye. And we were very down-to-earth. We were just bred for the law; we couldn't help it. It was basically in our blood ever since our grandfather.

Adele had finally taken a breath, but her chest was still heaving as I sat on the couch continuing to hang my head between my legs, only occasionally lifting my head to glance at everyone around the room. I realized Adele had lost her mind as well. This was bad but more for our parents. I didn't want them to drop dead from the shame and embarrassments from our huge fall from grace. We were prominent but having a chink in our armor per se was not going to ruin us. What it would do is give the people who hate us a chance to thumb their nose at us and tell us how we're not so goody-goody after all, though we never proclaimed to be. And of course we would be the butt of some good jokes for some time to come, but never to our faces. That's where being prominent came in to help big time, they always wanted your money or backing for something and they wouldn't risk ever losing that. Or they might have to come before you in court. No, they would never risk that.

"Evelyn, what are we going to do?" Did I hear correctly? Did someone just ask *ME* what we were going to do? I could swear it was Jackie, the instigator and ring leader of this problem and our parents imminent deaths. I pretended that I had not heard her, still hanging my head but I had begun to feel dizzy from the blood rush since I was no longer feeling as if I would pass out.

"Evelyn!" Jackie called out to me again.

"Jackieeeee!" I said stretching her name out in exasperation. "How am I supposed to know what to do?"

"Because you always figure things out and know what to do!" She pleaded back at me. Was she kidding?!! Who did she think I was?!! We had never encountered anything like this, I fixed little stuff like messed up plans or I helped figure people's financial issues out and that was only because I was organized and have a master's degree in finance.

I didn't go to law school, Jackie; you should be asking Gwen or Adele that question. I don't know what she possibly thought I could do, but I knew why she was looking to me. Just like I promised her I would handle the Yolanda and Michael issue though I was one hundred percent certain Michael was not cheating. I didn't know what he was doing but that I was sure about, but I'd always taken care of my little sister and been able to fix "it". If there were problems with her friends I helped work it out or if she spent all her money on clothes but still needed books, I bought them. Some years before we'd employed Janice, when Jackie was still a horrible cook but promised she'd be a great wife and mother and provide healthy home cooked meals, it was I who made double portions of everything so she could pretend she was actually making good meals. And unless she'd told Michael how we'd kept his stomach happy when they were first married, I'd never told a soul.

Jackie was set on marrying Michael before she graduated from college which was against Daddy's rules, but he didn't want her eloping and stealing the joy of giving her a big wedding from our mother. Daddy made her sign a contract stipulating that for him to give his blessing on her marriage and to give her the wedding she and mama dreamed about she had to not only graduate from college but she had to get her master's degree by the age of twenty five. Having children would be no excuse because he told her to hire a nanny. I do not know what the penalty was if she didn't hold to the contract but she kept it. She never had time to cook or learn how to be a good wife and mother and that's how I ended up making double portion meals that she could pass off as her own. She hired a housekeeper after she had her first baby. She still put so much trust in me, it hurt to look at her and see that she truly believed I could figure something out and fix this. This time I just didn't know where to begin.

Chapter Twelve

"Get me a drink, a stiff one!" I said to no one in particular but Katherine went to get me something nevertheless. When she handed me my drink I downed it in one swallow. It burned, but I didn't care; I wanted another one. Was I going to turn into an alcoholic? I didn't know, and at that moment I didn't care. I kept picturing Mama and Daddy seeing us on the news getting arrested, and then dropping dead from the shock. "Katherine, get me another drink, please." Once she returned with my second drink I sipped on that one.

"So, Ms. Jacqueline Lawrence," I glanced at Adele when I spoke. "Oh sorry, Ms. Jacqueline Isaacs-Lawrence. And I'm married to a judge, not a lawyer." Adele gave me the most chilling look, but I ignored it. I turned back to face Jackie. "How did you know that Anne's husband would be out of where they were staying for the period of time it took you to commit so many felonies?" Jackie, looked ashamed when I said the last part, as she should. The criminal!

"I overheard him talking to that woman about their plans for the day and evening, they chartered a helicopter to Memphis for a concert tonight, staying overnight there, and then returning tomorrow."

"I heard that, and all of a sudden I couldn't think. I just got so mad and just thought of Michael being with that Yolanda, and I lost it. I didn't stop to think until after I did it all. I'm really sorry everyone. I didn't mean to cause so much trouble. I would never hurt any of you on purpose. I just wasn't thinking."

"You can say that again." I heard Sheila mumble under her breath.

"And why are your fingerprints on bleach bottles when you were wearing gloves?" That question had been rattling around in my head since Adele had first said what Jackie had done.

"I took them off because I didn't want to get bleach on my gloves; I just bought them." We all just stared at her. Of all the reasons she could have had, she had to name what had to be the most chicken- headed reason there was. Apparently none of us knew what to say after that admission; we just continued to stare.

"Well, I don't know what to do about all that's happened, but I know what needs to be done here." I said to Jackie and Adele. "You two need to make up and apologize. There is no way you will let this come between you or any of us. I don't want to go to jail either, but we are still family and no one died. This is not worth losing each other over." Adele could hold a grudge, but she could just climb down off her big Isaacs' high horse and get over it. The damage had been done, and Jackie's stress over Michael was causing her to lose all common sense and rational thinking.

"Adele, I'm so sorry. I'm sorry to everyone here and all our family when this gets out. Please forgive me!" Adele said nothing, she was still frothing. We all said we forgave her and gave her a hug, everyone except for Gwen and Adele.

"Well," Gwen said, holding a hand towel that Katherine had given her once the fighting had stopped up to her face. "It's not a matter of forgiving you; I did that already. But one or both of you better apologize to me for punching me in the face. I don't know which one of you did it so you both need to tell me you're sorry."

"I'm so sorry, I didn't mean it." Jackie said in a pleading tone. "Thank you all for forgiving me." We all looked at Adele who still had said nothing.

"Adele?" I said. "What do you think would hurt Daddy more? That we all were arrested or that we did not stick together like he raised us to do?" She still was not budging. "Whether this comes out or not, do you want me to tell Daddy how you slapped Jackie and how you both were fighting?" Her face cringed at the thought.

"Fine!" Adele said as if it were costing her a million dollars to say. "I forgive you; and Gwen I'm sorry too if I punched you." Gwen and Jackie hugged and tried to pull Adele in, but she kept her arms to her sides still mad. Facing Daddy with the truth of that, was a lot worse than holding a grudge or being arrested; I knew that and I would tell!

Glancing at the clock, I realized that between all this craziness and my sleeping, it had been over four hours and I was starving.

"What do we have to eat? I'm really hungry as I'm sure all of us are or should be." Drinking on an empty stomach wasn't working for me either; I was starting to feel a bit drunk.

"Before they came back and started acting like wild animals, I made shrimp and it's still in the oven." Gwen told us. "I only now need to make the garlic bread and salad."

"I'll make the salad and set the table," said Ava.

"Jackie, why don't you and Adele get cleaned up. You both look a mess, especially your hair. And your make-ups' all smudged," I told both of them smiling. The mood needed to be lightened. Anymore crying and fighting and I was going home. They were driving me nuts!

Chapter Thirteen

Lunch actually ended up being pleasant. We put on some more music as we ate Gwen's marvelous shrimp salad and strawberries with whipped cream. I had been doing some thinking as well. Apparently, my silence and lack of participation in the conversations were noticed.

"What are you thinking about Evelyn?" Ava asked me. I heard her, but not really. I was lost in thought as I got up and walked into the other room looking for pen and paper. This, of course, got everyone's attention.

"Evelyn? Evelyn?" I still heard her, but I was too caught up in my own thoughts to respond. I was writing my list by this time.

"What is wrong with you?" Adele asked me as she came and gave me a little shake.

"I'm fine, just thinking. Jackie, when did you say Anne's husband said he would be returning?" I turned to Jackie when I received no response. She was opening and closing her mouth like a fish. I realized my question had just come out of the blue. "Jackie!" I snapped.

"Uh, well he just said in the morning!" She finally was able to speak.

"Was his hotel room in the ski lodge?"

"No, it was close, but not actually at the lodge. I had run over there, maybe a half mile in one direction. He's rented one of those smaller chalets."

"And what did you do with the key you stole from housekeeping?"

"I put it back on one of those carts. Why?" Jackie asked me and the others were staring at me with the same question mark on their faces.

"Because we're going to go back and delete the footage on the camera with Jackie in them and get that container with her fingerprints!"

"WHAT!!!!" They all screamed. That actually caused me to jump a little; I hadn't expected them to be so loud.

"You've got to be kidding me!" Katherine said. She was staring at me as if I had suddenly grown two heads. I looked over at Jackie and her face showed fear mingled with hope. "There is no way that I am going there!" Katherine yelled.

"Yes, you are!" I yelled back. "No one wants to get arrested and be on the news. And with the mess Jackie made, this is definitely going to come out. Getting arrested and being on the news is exactly what will happen. And Katherine if you don't do this with us, I will tell the authorities that you drove the getaway car for Jackie."

"Evelyn, you'd never." She countered angrily.

"Oh yes I will. Jackie is my sister. And even though she has created this mess we all are going to get her out of it. Since you will be sitting in jail right along with us you might as well help." I wasn't willing to hear any crap and they knew it by my face and voice. Adele actually looked excited. I'm sure she never saw herself committing a crime, especially multiple felonies, but she'd do just about anything to not let what happened get out and embarrass her. Apparently she was willing to commit more crimes to cover up the first ones. If I wasn't her sister I could blackmail her.

Gwen and Ava would go along regardless because I knew they would never let me or Jackie go alone. I had shut Katherine up so all that was left was Sheila and Anne. And Anne better not think about not going since this was partly her fault as well. It was her no-good-cheating-husband that was here with another woman. It must have been the look on my face because as soon as I turned to her she immediately agreed.

"Sheila?" I asked.

"Of course, I'm good to go. I'd rather get in trouble trying to fix it than just sitting here waiting for the police to come."

"First," I instructed them. "Sheila, I need for you and Ava to go and buy us some skull masks to cover our faces and jackets and pants and leather gloves. Try to find white or the lightest colors you can find but nothing neon. With all that snow we need to try and blend in as much as possible."

"Oh like camouflage." Gwen said with an enthusiasm I wasn't expecting.

"I can't believe you actually expect us to participate in a crime." Katherine said while wringing her hands.

"Well, believe it, because we are." I told her. "Also, find us some white snow boots if possible. There should be a lot of ski supply stores around because of the resort. Jackie you go with them so that you all can buy a few items each. I don't want all of the things we need on one persons credit card. We need flashlights as well, nice size ones not those little pen lights. You all need to go before it gets too dark so hurry up and finish eating."

After they left to shop for the night's upcoming events, I was in the kitchen cleaning up when Katherine came in. She didn't say anything just watched me.

"What is it Katherine?"

"Why are you being so mean, Evelyn? You threatened me!" I continued cleaning the stove as she spoke but had to turn and face her.

"Katherine you are my sister-in-law and I love you. I'm sorry that you feel that I was being mean, but I never threatened you." I again turned around and continued to clean the stove.

"But Evelyn how can you say that? You said you would tell the press that I helped Jackie do what she did." This time I didn't turn around, I just grabbed the broom and started sweeping.

"Yes, I did; but it wasn't a threat, it was a promise. Katherine, how long have you known me?"

"Over thirty years, but what.."

"When have I ever threatened anyone? I interrupted her. When I say I will do something I will do it, and we all need to stick together. If we were at home I would say Katherine go on home and we will take care of it, but we are in Tennessee in the mountains far away from home. So you can't just go home so we need to stick together."

"I think you understand why and will also agree with my plans once you've calmed down, you are just bothered by my words and my presumed anger at you. I wasn't angry. I was just defending what we have to do for all of us. Now go on and lie down for a while and rest." I continued to sweep as I heard her leaving the room. I understood she was afraid. I myself was terrified!

Chapter Fourteen

Knowing my plan could fail big time I found myself really wanting to be with Tony so I decided to call him to help ease my nerves. After a couple of rings he answered. "Hello baby, are you having a good time?" He asked me. His deep voice was music to my ears.

"Yes, I am. I was just missing you and wanted to call you." He laughed lightly.

"I missed you too, but I didn't want to interrupt any of your fun time with everyone."

"You know you can call me anytime; you would never interrupt me. So what are you doing anyway?"

"I'm on my way to visit my mom."

"Good; well tell her I said hello and that I'm thinking of her."

"I'll do that but how about we take her out to dinner when you get back."

"Sure, we can do that. She doesn't get out much anymore." Tony's mother was named Angela. She was eighty-three years old and in fact she didn't want to get out. After his father died, she didn't want to do anything more than watch the home shopping network and buy everything that caught her eye. We went over there every other month just for the purpose of collecting her ill-gotten gains and taking them to Goodwill as donations. She lived in the most expensive retirement community in the city so she didn't have to do anything for herself and she loved it. They had a concierge, maid service and an on staff chef that made all your meals and if she didn't want to go to the dining room to mingle with the other residents they brought it to her apartment. The place was great but getting her to leave when it wasn't a holiday was a job and a half.

"So what have you all been doing?" Tony asked me.

"Oh not too much, we took skiing lessons today. It was exhausting and fun. We've been shopping of course, and just having a good time in general. Talking, eating, drinking." I told him how Katherine only managed to fall all day. I had him laughing pretty hard with that vacation update.

"Babe, I've made it to my mother's so I need to let you go for now."

"Okay, well I will talk to you tomorrow. I love you Tony."

"I love you too." I hung up with Tony and decided to take my own advice except I'd had enough sleep so I decided to watch a movie.

They returned when my movie was ending and they seemed to be in good spirits while being weighted down with all the bags. We laid everything out on the pool table in the game room, they actually had purchased eight white snow suits which was smart thinking because the temperature had dropped drastically and it was freezing outside. "Well, it looks like we have everything we need, I hope." I told them. By this time everyone was in the room waiting for me to instruct them. Oh the pressure I had put on us, especially myself! "Listen everyone, I don't really know what we are doing or exactly how we are going to do it since I have never broken in anywhere either or done anything close to this. I just know we need to do this together and we will figure it out." I was doing my best not to let my fear show. "Let's leave all this stuff here, fix dinner and while we eat we can plan how we're going to do everything." Everyone agreed that was a good plan of action.

"I got it." Sheila said as she walked in the kitchen a little while later holding a map.

"Oh good, let me look at it." Adele said as she took the map of the ski resort from Sheila.

"It has all the chalets on the property as well." Sheila said. "Jackie point out which one is theirs." Adele laid the map out across the kitchen table and we all bent to look over it.

"This looks like the one they are staying in. It's the fifth chalet and looking at the key each inch equals a quarter of a mile, so from the chalet it's approximately two miles from the resort." Sheila seemed to be really getting into our caper of sorts. "Jackie, how long did it take you to get there and back?"

"Only about forty five minutes." We all just stared at her in shock!

"We know that you run but were you in a race?" Sheila asked incredulously. "You stole the key, ran two miles to the cabin, found scissors, cut up their clothes and then ran two more miles back?

"In forty five minutes and in the snow?!!" Adele asked her. I was in shock as well.

"I just ran, I knew I couldn't be gone too long or Ava and Anne would have gotten worried or suspicious." Jackie did a quick look at us around the room when she said that one. Yeah we knew suspicious was the proper word.

"How about we leave around midnight and take just one SUV, that way we'll definitely all be together, less conspicuous and there won't be many people around." I suggested still managing to sound in control.

"Anne, we have never asked how you feel about all of this. I mean I know we have to do this to save Jackie's bacon and to protect our parents but it is your husband that is staying here with another woman. So, how do you feel?" I asked her.

At first she didn't say anything while she sat down at the table, the rest of us were still standing. She took a deep breath and then it seemed to all just come spilling out.

"I really don't know how I feel." Anne began. "Except that things have been bad for quite some time now. It hurts but it doesn't surprise me that he's cheating. I've only ever worked part time at the library, I've only been a housewife and mother all my life but I was always given an allowance for my own personal things like hair appointments, getting my nails done; things like that. I never shopped much but I was able to shop when I wanted. I knew what we could afford and not afford so I always shopped within our budget. About eight months ago we seemed to start arguing about things that made no sense, and if I asked him questions he told me to mind my own business, that it was none of my business or to just leave him alone. I gained a few pounds and he started pointing it out and calling me fat so I tried to diet and exercise but I wasn't losing any weight. He took my credit cards and told me I wasn't going to just waste his money buying all new clothes when I was being lazy and just not losing the weight."

Anne was speaking in an unnatural calmness, I'm no psychiatrist but her emotion just didn't seem normal and looking around the room at the duplicate expressions of anger and outrage on everyone's faces I reinforced my thoughts and feelings on this.

And Anne was not fat, a bit overweight but far from fat. I couldn't stand no good men.

"I still work part time so I've been able to buy a few items of clothing and I can still wear most of my clothes, they are mainly just too tight. When Jackie brought up this trip I knew I could never afford it and asking Brian was out of the question. I didn't want to admit that I couldn't afford to go and that my husband had slowly been turning into another person but when Jackie offered to pay I let my pride go because I truly wanted to come and I needed to get away. I couldn't have imagined in my wildest dreams that Brian would be at the same place we've come for a vacation and at the exact same time, that just doesn't seem possible but nevertheless it has happened. After all of this I know a divorce is inevitable and I want one but I don't want to lose my house but I can't afford to keep it up and I can't afford a good lawyer or a lawyer period. I'm sure he will file soon, then I will have nothing, I don't have minor children for child support and I'm not trained to do anything. What an idiot I've been, never going to school to learn a job skill, believing we would be together forever and he would always take care of me." Anne still sounded calm but a spirit of defeat seemed to have taken over her; she was more than calm she was monotone.

Ava walked over in front of Anne, knelt so her face was at the same level as Anne's and reached around her neck and hugged her so hard it had to have hurt.

I knew we were all feeling the same, but Ava was the extremely affectionate one with everyone and nearly anyone so her reaching out to hug Anne as if she was her dearest friend was a normal thing for her. For the rest of us, it took more time. We were more of "I'll write you a check to make you feel better" women. Anne was a bit shocked because she didn't really know Ava or any of us except for Jackie of course.

"Anne," Ava said in a soothing and calm voice after she finally let her go. "First of all it is not idiotic to believe your husband would always be faithful and support his family; you are his family. Never believe that. Second it is honorable to be a homemaker, to raise your children and take care of your husband and home. And third and last, your sister-in-law has nothing but attorneys in her family with three of them in this very room. Well two, because I'm a tax attorney and try never to deal with people outside of that realm. However, you have shown Jackie a disservice because you have allowed her to pay for a trip but you have not spoken up to her to help you with the poor excuse for a husband he obviously has become. If you are ashamed of anything then that is the one thing you should be ashamed of." Anne had begun to cry.

I swear to God I didn't think I could take anymore crying! What was wrong with them; couldn't they hold a single conversation this trip without crying and being sad? I thought to myself.

"Jackie, I'm sorry." Anne cried. "I wasn't trying to treat you any less that you are, I swear. I am just so ashamed and I never thought to think that your family would help me like that. Legal fees can be so expensive and to expect your family to help a practical stranger would be taking advantage of you and your family." Ava sat down next to Anne and faced her.

"Anne, listen to me. You're right. Your shame kept you from saying anything but Jackie has been married to your brother for almost thirty years which means she's been your sister-in-law for the same amount of time. Knowing how kind, caring and giving Jackie is, I'm happy to hear you didn't want or try to take advantage of her. You also know because of her nature that she loves and cares about you. You were right to think we may not help because we don't know you, but Jackie would have given or loaned you the money to go to any attorney you wanted. But to not trust or confide in her; I know Jackie; and this hurts her. I also know that she forgives you and I can speak for Adele and Gwen, one of them will take your case and be your attorney, but you don't have to go to them; you can still hire any attorney that you want and Jackie will pay for it." Ava was so freely giving Jackie's money away which would never work for me but she hadn't spoken out of turn, we all knew Jackie would give her the money. I could tell Anne was overwhelmed with emotions. Jackie and Anne hugged while Anne continued to whisper apologies to her and Jackie telling her in reply that they weren't needed.

"And, of course I want one of you to handle my case please; I know you're the best." Anne said now smiling but with tears still flowing.

"Anne! Gwen said from across the table. When we get back home we will file for the divorce and trust me you will get to keep your house and have the money to afford to take care of it and yourself."

"But how?" Anne stammered.

"Will you just trust me? I got this. We'll talk about it at my office when we get back." Gwen promised. "Call the office to make an appointment first thing when we get home."

"I don't know what to say, I can't believe you're willing to do this for me." Anne said in an awed but dazed voice.

"For now think no more about it; we have more than enough ahead of us tonight." Gwen could always put things back on track.

Chapter Fifteen

After dinner, more talking and trying in vain to rest. It was now time to head out, and boy were we nervous. Actually, terrified was a more accurate word. We walked outside and the cold and force of the wind practically knocked us down and made icicles out of us at the same time.

"It's freezing out here; we should have warmed the truck up first," Sheila said.

"You're right. But we're out here now, so let's hurry up and get in." I told them, my voice already beginning to tremble from the cold. As we piled in with Ava at the wheel we did not fit comfortably since this was a seven passenger and we were eight.

"Evelyn, thank goodness you are skinny or we might not fit," Sheila told me as we squeezed in. I detested being called skinny especially since all my sisters were slim, but this was a tense situation so I kept my emotions on that locked down.

"It's pitch black out here; I can't see a thing." Ava said as she inched the truck along. I sat in the back once again praying that we did not drive off the road and off the mountain plummeting to our deaths. What would normally take five minutes to drive down from our chalet to the main road in daylight took us twenty-five minutes to drive down in the middle of the night in complete darkness. It was about twenty degrees but by the time we made it to the main road we were all glistening in sweat. We all gave a collective thank you God as soon we made it. We began to relax a little on the way towards the ski resort but the closer we got our tension level began to rise once more. I could practically smell the fear from everyone.

"Park on the far side of the building." I told Ava. "Let's all go in. It will look strange for any of us to be sitting out here in the cold. The lobby and bar area are open twenty-four hours so there should be people there even at this hour of the morning. Once we go in the rest of you pretend to get comfortable and sit at the bar and drink some hot chocolate or whatever while Jackie and I go searching for the keys."

As we all walked into the lobby it was full of people even at one in the morning. People were surrounding the huge fire place, it reminded me of something straight out of a book. The fireplace was in the middle of the room and was open to both sides; it went all the way to the ceiling and in fact was so large I'm sure I could stand up in it. It had beautiful stones covering it. It split the room into two, one side being the bar and lounge and the other side the restaurant. I could even see through to the restaurant and that appeared to be open as well. The rooms were decorated very comfortably in large leather sofas and chairs in rich colors of blues and browns. The only thing I thought was hideous but I supposed it fit a ski resort in the mountains was a huge chandelier made with what looked like animal bones of some kind. I saw there were only three available stools available at the bar.

"Adele, Katherine and Ava sit at the bar. Sheila, Gwen and Anne go sit at the fireplace. The waiter will come around to take your orders. Here, take my coat." I said as I handed it to Adele. "Jackie, give her yours too."

"Why are you taking off your coat?" Katherine asked still with a terrified look on her face.

"Because we need to look like we are here to just hang out like everyone else. And Katherine, stop looking like you're about to be arrested, relax or at least try and look relaxed." She visibly tried to relax but it didn't work. Oh well she tried. I walked up to the bar behind Ava.

"Excuse me sir." I beckoned to the bartender. He was a handsome man looking about thirty five and since I only looked to be about forty I gave him the most flirtatious smile I had in my arsenal of flirting. This part was easy since I flirted with Tony all the time, lots of practice. It worked; he was grinning right back at me.

"Hi, I lost my key to my cabin. Can you tell me where I can go to get a copy at this time of the morning?"

"Yeah you can go down to the security office in the basement." He told me pointing in the opposite direction of where we came in.

"Thank you so much." I laid a syrupy tone laying it on thick.

"May I buy you a drink?" The handsome bartender asked.

"That would be great but I really need to get to the security office to get a copy of my key; I'm very tired and should get to bed." He actually looked disappointed. Wow! I still had it.

"Well, my name is Kevin so if you change your mind, I'm here all night."

"I'll remember that. Thanks again, Kevin." I said giving him a wink as I turned away.

"Come on Jackie." I said while taking her arm to walk down the hall towards the stairs.

"Evelyn you were so flirting with him." She said smiling at me. I had obviously entertained her.

"Of course I was, remember you catch more flies with honey. Men love it when you smile and I did along with a little flirting. That's how I landed Tony."

"Oh please, he was hooked as soon as he saw you."

"Well, that's how I keep him." When we got down to the security office we saw there was a security officer at a desk with a lot of camera screens. We walked to the end of the hallway so we could talk without being heard.

"We need to get him out of there somehow, I saw a door marked keys as we passed by. I told Jackie in a whisper. But I'm sure if we manage to get him out he will lock the door and we need to be able to get in that door and I'm going to assume the doors with the keys are locked as well."

Jackie looked down the hall once more towards the security office.

"The door opens out so possibly we can get the hinge off the door. But we need something to work with." Jackie said whispering.

"I have an idea." I told her as I reached in my pocket for my phone and called Ava. After two rings Ava answered.

"Hey, how's it going so far down there?" She asked me excitedly but in a hushed voice.

"Not so good, listen there is a small toolbox that the rental company put in the truck. I need you to go get it and meet me on the rear stairs. Have Adele do something that will make the guy in the security office leave so we can get in."

"Okay." She answered, but I stopped her before she could hang up.

"Ava wait. Have Adele do whatever she needs to do before you meet me. That way the guy will already be gone. Make sure to tell Adele that he needs to leave the building. Once you see him leave then text me so we can meet you in the stairwell. We need to hide somewhere. We've already been in this hallway too long."

"What do I tell her to do?" Ava asked.

"I don't know! Just anything that would need security outside." I was getting agitated but not with her just the situation in general. I was completely out of my element and I needed to not freak out. Jackie looked at me strangely when I told Ava what I wanted with Adele. Jackie didn't understand; Adele could be the meanest drama queen in designer clothes but was tough as nails and the best to remain calm under pressure. And she was super smart; she would think of something.

Jackie and I went back upstairs but bypassed the lobby floor to be safe and went to the second floor and hid out in a public bathroom in the restroom stall.

"What's taking so long?" Jackie asked while sitting on the toilet with her elbows on her knees and her head in her hands. Her feet wouldn't stop tapping the floor; she was beginning to make me nervous.

"Jack, it's only been ten minutes and we have barely begun. Do not flip out on me now." We were both in the same stall with me standing leaning against the door and her constant movements made me feel more cramped. I knew she couldn't control her nervousness so asking her to stop would have been pointless.

"Ev, I'm sorry. I know I just can't seem to stop thinking it's not going to work."

"Stop that negative thinking right now. It's going to work; it has to. There's no other choice." Of course I knew no such thing but I refused to believe that I risked my life coming down that mountainside in the pitch black night for nothing. All of a sudden we heard what sounded like multiple car alarms going off. Jackie and I looked at one another and I knew I had the identical smile on my face that I saw on hers.

"Way to go Adele!" Jackie said beginning to stand up.

"No," I stopped her, "we have to wait for Ava's text." We only had to wait another two minutes before Ava's text came through telling us to meet her on the stairs. We hurried to the steps and got the toolbox from Ava.

"Let us know if you see him returning before we get back upstairs." She nodded, and hurried back as soon as I took the toolbox from her.

"Ready, let's get started." I had no-in depth knowledge of tools but if I had to break the door down that's what I was willing to do. "Jackie, no matter how much I watch television, I'm pretty sure I won't be any good at picking a lock so the tweezers are out." I said while we looked at the contents of the toolbox.

"Are tweezers standard for a toolbox anyway?" she asked me.

"I don't know, I know as much as you or less when it comes to using anything other than hammer and nails." We could still hear the alarms going off. It actually sounded like more than before. Whatever Adele was doing it was obviously working. "We need to hurry since we know we can't pick the lock; your idea of taking the hinges off the door seems to be our best option. You take this flathead screwdriver, place it on the hinge and I will hammer the head to lift it out." I told Jackie and she immediately grabbed the screwdriver and did as I instructed.

"I hoped they are well lubed," she said.

"Me too!"

My first whack with the hammer was a total failure; I missed the screwdriver completely but nailed Jackie's hand. Jackie screamed so loud I was sure people would come running to see what was wrong. I dropped the hammer and reached for her.

"Oh my God, I'm so sorry, so, so sorry." I said over and over while I held her. Her sobs finally subsided, she lifted her head and looked me straight in the eyes and spoke quite calmly for someone in such pain.

"Come on let's try again!"

Chapter Sixteen

After that horrific first attempt we were actually making headway but the racket we were making had us in constant fear of being caught. I knew the pain in Jackie's hand had to be killing her by the way she wouldn't and couldn't use it and the strain on her face that didn't come from the fear in her eyes but from pain, but she never complained or said a word. I was amazed and proud at the same time of her inner strength to persevere. The first hinge popped out. "Yay," she cheered quietly. One down two to go. We immediately began on the second one which came out easier than the first. We were making great time and the alarms were still going off. The third hinge is where we got stuck!

"Jackie, I'm going to have to do this one by myself but you hold the door just in case it starts to fall."

"I'm hot!" She said sweating with the pain from her hand and I felt so bad. I hoped it wasn't broken. The last hinge was so low to the floor getting the right angle to push it up was nearly impossible. I knelt on the floor trying to do this and I couldn't tell if it was my age or the concrete floors but my knees were killing me.

"This hinge has not been kept lubed like the others ones." I told Jackie as I hammered and pushed up with the screwdriver consecutively. I began to sweat as well from my exertion of trying to force the hinge to move. I rolled over on my back deciding this would be a better angle to be able to push from. I was right, it was hard but it was finally moving.

"You almost have it!" Jackie said just as the hinge popped out. I just lay there for a few seconds trying to catch my breath. Getting up, I realized I was now filthy.

"So much for blending in!" I said.

"You're fine; let's just hurry up and get in." Jackie said, while using her good hand to help me up while leaning on the door just in case it came loose from the frame and fell on us. I put the hammer back in the toolbox but still kept the screwdriver.

I'm going to wedge the screwdriver between the door and the frame to give us leverage so we can pull the door out. We found out quickly that pulling the door was unnecessary, as soon as I able to wedge the screwdriver in the door fell on us. It was so heavy it knocked us into the opposite wall but because the hallway was not as wide as the door was long it trapped us.

"Agh!" We both cried out in surprise and a bit of pain as the door slammed into us.

"We need to get this door off of us! Jackie cried. And it weighs a ton."

"Oh God! I cried while trying to push the door off of us. Jackie, lets push together on three."

"All right." She readily agreed.

"One, we counted together. Two! Three!" We shoved, but to no avail, the door barely budged an inch.

"Oh God, oh God, Oh God! What are we going to do?" Jackie was starting to panic.

"Don't panic, let me think! We can't lift the door; we're going to have to go under it. Since it's laying on a slant there's a small space that we should be able to fit through. Just slide down the wall and crawl out." She began sliding down and when she made it to the bottom she got on her knees and crawled. It was harder because of her hand, but she made it out.

"Evelyn, now you!" I slid down and crawled out behind her.

"Let's get in the office. Jackie, you get the keys and I'll work on the security video." The door was on a slant like a slide so we climbed on the door and slid into the office.

We caught one break tonight, the key closet was unlocked and I was betting that the security officer was in a rush to get to the chaos Adele caused that he didn't bother to sign off the computer and I was right. "Jackie, we're in!" There were rows of plastic key cards in a glass case so she had already located the copy of the key card where Brian the jerk and his floozy were staying, but she had found some scissors and were destroying the others as well so they wouldn't know which was missing.

The security program they used was very standard so I was able to find the video footage of the previous day where Jackie was caught clear as day stealing from housekeeping. As well as the footage of us this very night in the stairwell and in the hall breaking in. I deleted the footage and all the history but to insure it was completely gone I set the hard drive back to system settings. I located their back up hard drive and repeated the process. To be on the extra safe side I logged onto a website that I knew would attack their system with a worm or virus after typing in a few strokes I had learned when I had decided to take a simple programming class in computer design. Learning about viruses and worms was not a part of the class and was way above our scope of learning but our teacher was a young twenty-something computer enthusiast who couldn't help himself but to show us how to do bad things as well. I was always a great student and I took good notes. I noticed that their system was extremely weak which wasn't exactly surprising. A ski resort wouldn't need super high tech security but they would probably rethink that after they found what we had done.

"I've deleted everything and reset their system so the cameras are dead until they reprogram! You ready?"

"Yes! Let's go." Jackie said following me out the door.

We climbed back over the door to get out of the office and ran so fast up the stairs we were practically flying. We decided to go back up to the second floor and took the elevator down to the lobby rather than coming out the stairs where we might be remembered later. We walked back into the main lobby and bar area and spotted Ava, Adele and Katherine sitting at the bar the same as when I left them. As I glanced at my watch I couldn't believe the time! Miraculously we had only been gone about thirty minutes, it felt like a lifetime. "Jackie, go get the others and head to the car, I'll get the ones at the bar and we'll be out to meet you in about five minutes."

"Alright!" I watched her as she walked up to the large fireplace that had bar tables up close to it, Gwen handed her her coat and I watched as she gathered the others and left. I walked and stood next to Ava and smiled at Kevin who was still attending bar.

"You ready to let me buy you that drink?" He asked me.

"I'm sorry Kevin I wish I were but I've been here longer than planned already and need to be on my way. But can I get a cup filled with ice please?" They each looked at me with a puzzled expression. "I'll explain later." As I was putting on my coat Kevin gave me the cup of ice. "Thank you," I smiled at him then walked out.

Walking outside there were people everywhere but only one police car that I could see of. I had nearly forgotten about the mishap going on out here that Adele has created for us.

"Adele!" I said in astonishment. "What did you do?" She grinned at us.

"I'll tell you in the truck." As we walked around to the side of the building where we parked the SUV, I saw Gwen at the wheel with it turned on ready to go. We piled in but I told Gwen not to drive off yet.

"Here Jackie, I got this ice for your hand."

"Oh thank you." She said and immediately plunged her hand in the cup of ice. Does anyone have any pain pills?" Jackie said as she simpered in pain while holding her hand in the cup of ice.

"We left our purses at the chalet. Gwen told her. But what happened to your hand?"

"Evelyn hit it with the hammer!"

"Ouch!" Ava said.

"It hurt a lot more than ouch. Will someone please find me something for the pain?" Jackie screamed.

"Oh, I remember." Katherine said. "We have the little medicine kit in the back. Gwen, open the tailgate so I can get it." Katherine said as she got out the truck and was back it seemed within seconds. "Here's a bottle of ibuprofen. How many do you want?" She asked Jackie.

"All of them!" Jackie screamed again. Katherine looked at her and shook out a few. "You can have four, and then a few more in a couple of hours" Jackie snatched them out of her hand threw them in her mouth along with cubes of ice from her cup and swallowed everything whole.

"Okay everyone," I said. "Let's regroup before we head to the cabin."

"They are in cabin six so let's park near number four; just in case we are spotted no one needs to see the truck as well. We'll also remove the license plates for the same reason. This should be a piece of cake compared to what we just had to go through. It shouldn't take us more than a few minutes to get in through a window, get the container and get out then be back on our way. Then we can take Jackie to a hospital; Gwen, let's go."

"No wait!" Jackie said holding her hand tight to her chest. She was in so much pain she could barely speak; her lips didn't seem to be moving and she was sucking in gulps of air.

"Wait? Jackie we have to go." Katherine said in annoyance.

"I want to know what Adele did to cause all this mayhem for us first!" Jackie said now trembling in pain.

"What!!! Jackie!!!" We all shrieked at her.

"Jackie, we have to go, obviously the pain is affecting your brain." Adele said sounding totally exasperated. "I will tell it on the way; Gwen get a move on." When Adele gave that order in the drill sergeant voice Gwen put the truck in gear and slammed on the gas.

"Slow down!" We all screamed! "Just drive normal." Sheila screamed.

"Sorry," she replied while slowing down to a normal speed.

"Well Adele what happened?" Jackie was a like a dog with a bone, she wouldn't let wanting to know go.

"Fine!" Adele said. "When Ava first told me Evelyn wanted me to do something to cause a distraction I had no idea what to do, and of course I didn't want to get caught doing what I hadn't yet come up with. The only thing I noticed right away that we had going in our favor was the weather. It's so cold outside that no one was hanging around; they went in quickly and went out just as fast. Still not knowing what I was going to do, I enlisted Gwen to go with me. I needed to keep Ava and Katherine at the bar to hold my seat and so it wouldn't look weird if we all got up together, the security is needed and then we all just come strolling back in together. No; that wouldn't look suspicious now would it?!"

"Since it's freezing out here we were able to use our ski mask to cover our faces. We jogged around the building to the parking lot where we came to parking area the guest that are staying here in the actual resort are using." As Adele told us the story her voice became more animated. "I decided I needed the alarms to go off so we both found a brick and Gwen went down one row and I the other and broke the driver side windows reached in and open the doors."

"Why did you need to open the doors?" Asked Katherine.

"Because just breaking the windows won't make the alarms go off but since the doors are locked with a remote not using the remote to open the door makes the alarm go off. You should have seen us hustle, it was actually fun." Adele gave a quiet sigh with a huge smile on her face. "I do feel a bit bad about breaking all those people's windows though, especially since I'm an officer of the court and I'm supposed to obey the laws not break them, but it was their windows or us, so I broke them and kept going. I think we both set off about ten each, we knew that would keep security busy because they would have to locate the owners to get the alarms turned off then see if there is anything missing. And being on top of this mountain, unless it's a major crime they only have their private little security. Apparently all those car alarms freaked them out so they called the sheriff's department but it wasn't even Gatlinburg or Pigeon Forge Sheriff. The ski resort is called Deer Oak Ski Resort right?! Well they have their own little Deer Oak Sheriff's Department." Adele finished telling us in a smug tone.

"What are they, Mayberry?" I asked and we all laughed. We had finally made it to the turn off that led to the cabins. Once again it was pitch black; thank goodness we were not on a narrow mountain road, but there was the possibility of hitting a tree if we slid off the road somehow. In the Escalade and being assured it had the best snow tires on the market, that wasn't likely going to happen.

"Gwen, park over close to that cabin." I told her. "Close enough that it looks like we might be staying there but not too close that we can be heard in case the people inside wake up." As Gwen parked near the cabin and turned off the headlights, I reached on the floor to the trusty little toolbox I had used earlier that morning and retrieved the flathead screwdriver again.

"We're at cabin four, right?" I asked no one in particular.

"Yes!" Gwen said. "Cabin six should be about another quarter mile down the road."

"Evelyn, I'm scared." Katherine said.

"Me too!" Sheila, Gwen and Anne said in unison.

"It's pitch black out here," Katherine continued. I looked around at each of them. I noticed Jackie's face was still clinched in pain; she looked miserable.

"Katherine, give me that bottle of ibuprofen, please." She handed them to me; I shook out two more pills and handed them to Jackie. "Here, take two more. I'm so sorry. I promise we'll get to a hospital as soon as we get this done."

"I know, and it's okay." She managed to say while swallowing the pills, though it was obvious she was in agony. I had yet to respond to them and I knew they wanted me to tell them that they had nothing to be scared of, but I couldn't do that. I had never been so afraid in all my life, but we couldn't turn back now. So I decided to be half frank with them.

"I know everyone is afraid, but we can't turn back now. We have our flashlights and we'll take the toolbox just in case. I'll remove the license plates and then we'll head out. Jackie, Sheila and Katherine, you'll stay in the truck, the rest of us will go. Sheila, please get in the driver's seat and be ready to come get us if we call. Now, let me get the license plates off first and then we'll go." I told them as I got out of the truck. Ava got out of the car with me. I knew she would without having to ask. She turned on her flashlight so we could see as we walked to the back of the SUV. As I knelt down to work on the license plate, my hands began to shake and not from the frigid cold. At that moment I was so afraid of the unknown that I didn't know what to do. I was afraid of walking up that dark road, of going into that cabin. I was afraid that we would fail, but I couldn't let Jackie down, not my Jackie. And I couldn't let our parents find out we turned into criminals. Ava must have noticed how I was shaking because she knelt beside me and just held me for a moment until my shaking subsided.

I finished unscrewing the back plate and then did the front. I opened the door to the SUV, dropped the screws into the side pocket and laid the plates onto the floor. "Come on ladies, it's time to go!"

Chapter Seventeen

As Gwen, Adele, Ava, Anne and I walked down the pitch black road with only our magnum flashlights to light our paths and our trusty tool box, we made a very lonely picture. Five black women in the Tennessee Mountains, in the dead of winter, on foot in the middle of the night; we looked like a horror movie waiting to happen. The temperature was frigid, but that thought chilled me to my core.

"Evelyn, remind me to kill you when we get home." Gwen told me as we trudged along. "We are insane to be out here, I can't believe we let you talk us into this. You didn't do this for the family; you did this for Jackie! I mean, I know you love all of us, but when it comes to Jackie you just don't care; you seem willing to do anything for her, and us being out here proves it."

I couldn't believe what I was hearing, as I looked at her in my peripheral vision. Well, I could believe it, but not from Gwen. This is something I would have expected from Adele but obviously I had forgotten, for a moment how alike she and Adele were.

"If it were you who had caused this, I would still be out here and you know it." I defended myself, totally offended.

"I suppose you're right," she conceded. "But it's always about Jackie or Ava."

"Hey!" Ava interjected. "Leave me out of it."

"Listen," I said sarcastically. "When you are in jeopardy of going to jail for stealing, breaking and entering, and destruction of property, and you need help getting out of it. Give me a call. I promise I will walk in the middle of the woods for you too."

Gwen stopped and looked at me then burst out laughing. Soon the rest of us were laughing with her. We laughed for about five minutes; we couldn't seem to stop. The whole situation we had gotten ourselves in was so ridiculous that it seemed to just hit us all at once. We felt so much more at peace in spite of our situation. I could feel the last of our anger fall away, and we were best friends again.

We finally made it to the dreaded number six cabin of Brian, the cheater and the floozy. As soon as we got close to the front of the property, bright motion lights suddenly came on. At first we froze in shock before scattering like roaches when the lights come on. We all ducked behind trash cans.

"What in the world?" I said huffing from the shot of adrenaline to my system. "Why?" Huffing. "Would?" Huffing. "They have freaking flood lights?" Still huffing from the adrenaline the fear the floodlights caused.

"I really wasn't expecting that!" Ava said, breathing as heavily as I was.

"Hmm. We need to figure out how to get around those lights," I said.

"We're going to have to go back, and go around the back of that pole with the light on it, then hope there are no lights on the side." Adele said.

"But on the sides the windows are high up; we'll need something to stand on," Anne said. I then realized we were huddled behind the perfect step stools.

"We can use these trash cans; they should be tall enough." I told them. "But first we need to see if we can do it before we drag these cans over there. Adele, you and Ava try it first to make sure we can bypass the lights then come back." I told them. They readily agreed, nodding their heads.

"Ava, let's run it. The faster we find out, the faster we get it done and get out of here." Adele told her.

"Sounds like a plan, let's go." Ava said in return.

By this time, the floodlight had turned off and they grabbed hands and took off running. The rest of us were using our flashlights to follow them. They made it back to the main road and cut left to stay behind the pole. As they made the turn to head towards the side of the cabin, Ava slipped and fell.

"Oh no!" Anne screamed but Adele managed to stay on her feet despite holding Ava's hand and she pulled her up quickly. They barely seemed to slow down. This was one of the main reasons I wished I hadn't handicapped Jackie and had to leave her in the car. I didn't know what we might encounter but we all ran miles a day, not in the snow of course, but I knew we had the stamina to run or walk miles. I had nothing against Anne, but I had no idea if she could keep up, I knew Sheila and Katherine couldn't, but there was more safety in numbers so she had to come with us since Jackie couldn't.

They finally made it to the cabin and around the side without running into the line of the motion lights where they ended up out of our site.

"Where are they?" Gwen asked while swishing her flashlight around trying to find them.

"Oh there they are!" I caught the beam of their flashlight and saw them running headed back our way. When they finally made it back to us, they were smiling and barely breathing heavy.

"We made it!" Ava said excitedly. She apparently hadn't run long enough; she was jogging in place. I just shook my head and kept my mouth shut.

"It was a piece of cake, even though I did slip." We couldn't keep from smiling at her child-like exuberance over her run and fall. Again, I just smiled and shook my head.

"Let's grab a can; it's weighted so it doesn't blow away in the wind. We will have to drag it." I grabbed one handle and Anne grabbed the other side while Gwen and Adele led the way. Ava walked behind.

So far this was the hardest job of the night, even harder than trying to shove that door at the resort. The can was massive and it weighed a ton. We had to drag in shifts from the strain on our hands, and it was slow moving.

"Anne, watch out!" Ava yelled, but too late as Anne slipped and went down at the very same spot Ava had when she and Adele were running. But without someone holding her hand as Ava had with Adele, Anne kept moving or more accurately she kept sliding. The hill wasn't very steep, but it had a decent strip of ice. She hit it just at the very spot to career her forward. She didn't go too far, but she went very fast. She finally stopped when she grabbed a tree to stop her slide, but when she fell, it was our turn pulling the can again, and I couldn't hold onto it. When she went down, the force of her fall caused her to yank the can from me. It went rolling after her, and when she grabbed the tree to stop her decent, the trash can hit her in the back and slammed her head into the trunk of the tree. Her head against the tree gave a solid thwack sound.

"Oh my God!" We all screamed as we ran to her, trying not to fall ourselves.

"Anne, are you ok?" I asked,

"Uh, I think so." She said, sounding dazed.

I reached to grab her arm. "Help me pick her up! Adele, grab her other arm." We came up behind her. As soon as we lifted and turned her, we saw her face and gasped. Blood was gushing from her forehead and the lump was the size of a grapefruit. She looked deformed!

"What do we do?" Ava squealed in agitation. We all looked at one another in complete bewilderment. We knew business and the law; there wasn't a health care worker among us. The most we had ever done was wrap a sprained ankle or slapped a band aid on something. I was racking my brain trying to think up any possible solution.

"Oh," I said thinking of Jackie's hand. "We are in a bunch of snow. We can put it on her face for the swelling, and I think it will also stop the blood." I didn't know if it actually made sense and I knew that I was truly reaching but it was the best I had.

Adele and Gwen had reached down to grab snow before I finished getting the words out of my mouth. Anne grimaced in pain as Adele packed snow on her head, and Gwen was using the skull cap to mop up the blood.

"We need to try and get going again." I said. "Ava, help me pick up the trash can." We tried picking it up, but it was so heavy we couldn't right it completely without it rolling. We'd have to start over again. Gwen came over and helped us while Adele packed more snow on Anne's face. Adele looked like she was trying to freeze her face or she thought Anne was part snowman.

We finally got the trash can righted and settled, when I turned to see that Adele had gotten Anne standing, but walking straight wasn't going so well. Anne was toddling along looking like a baby taking her first steps. If this were a cartoon, birds would be flying over her head. I had to turn my head away or I was going to lose it again. I really didn't want to find humor in her pain and misery by laughing, but it was funny. Well, at least I didn't cause this one!

Chapter Eighteen

We finally got back on our way. Adele was Anne's crutch, while Ava, Gwen and I pulled and tugged the heavy can while trying to keep it balanced at the same time; thank God the lid was secured with some kind of new locking mechanism or trash would be all over the place. This was turning out to be the longest night of my life and already it was the worst. Tony would kill me if he knew I was out here like this in the middle of the night.

"Oh, we made it!" I told them while bending down trying to catch my breath after dealing with the physical war of the garbage can. Gwen and Ava seemed to be struggling to get their breath as well.

"I guess we should all start running with oversize weighted garbage cans from now on so we'll be ready the next time." Ava said panting. I gave her a little smile while Gwen burst out laughing then started coughing since she hadn't yet caught her breath completely. Gwen's coughing fit got Adele laughing; Anne seemed to be in too much pain to do much of anything except look miserable. She finally gained her balance and was walking straight, but she just stood holding packed snow to her head.

"Stop laughing. We only have to get in this cabin and get the bleach bottle and this godforsaken night can be over." I hushed them trying to get us back on track; I never wanted to go home so badly, be in my own bed next to my own husband.

"Gwen, help me pull the can under the window so Ava can climb up." I told her.

"Me!!!" Ava screeched. "I don't want to go in there."

"Yes, you! You and Adele climb up while Gwen and I make sure to keep the can stable." When I added this, Adele just put her hand on her hip and stared at me, but she didn't say anything. Gwen and I got the can as close to the building as we could. A lot of snow had fallen, so it wasn't the slightest bit steady and it was imperative that we held it up tight. "Ava, up you go!" She gave me the stink eye, but she climbed up on the teetering can.

"I'm going to fall." She said in a scared voice, as she slowly stood with one hand on the building and the other out at her side. She wobbled on the can as we tried our best to hold it steady on packs of snow and ice.

"No, you won't fall!" I tried to tell her in a confident voice. She stood directly under the window, but when she reached up for it she wasn't close enough.

"Oh crap, you're not tall enough," Adele cried out as she could see where we couldn't since we were directly under Ava, struggling and concentrating on making sure we held the can upright. She and Anne were standing away from the building watching. Why I had not thought of that I did not know; Ava was only five feet two.

"I'm not tall enough. Can't reach it, so I can't go in." Ava sounded way too happy with this turn of events. Then she just jumped off, slid in the snow a bit, but she was fine.

"I thought you were afraid of falling!" Gwen said, looking at Ava in disbelief after watching her dismount off the trash can.

"Yeah!" I said in agreement with Gwen.

"I was afraid of falling, not jumping." We all just looked at her then back at each other and just rolled our eyes.

"I'm game, I will do it." I told them realizing it had to be me or Gwen since we were both three inches taller but Gwen was heavier than I, she would do better helping to balance the can. "Ava help hold this can. Adele and I will climb up and go in." I said this while switching places with Ava and climbing up on the can, and yes, I was afraid I was going to fall as well, as I began wobbling, but I refused to admit it. As I balanced myself while starting to stand, I caught site of Anne out the corner of my eye. I know it was wrong and illogical to lay any blame on her for this predicament, but it was her husband that caused Jackie to be pushed over the edge of temporary insanity, and I just couldn't help myself but be a little mad at her. I also understood that I was being illogical to not hold blame to Jackie, but I just couldn't make myself. I wasn't perfect and I knew that about myself. In the back of my mind I knew she helped create this ridiculous situation, but I could not be mad with her for more than five minutes; I never could. It's very important to know one's own faults and loving my sisters beyond all reason was mine.

As I finally stood straight and reached up, I was able to reach the windowsill above me and since Adele was a little taller than I, I knew she would have no problem reaching it as well. All I had to do was hope I had enough upper body strength to lift myself until I could swing my legs up. Oh boy, I thought. This was going to be tough. I ran, I did not lift weights other than chubby grandbabies. I only had my thin, lightweight frame going for me. I still wasn't sure that would be enough!

"Adele," I called looking down at her. "I'm not sure I can pull myself up!"

"Yes you can." She said to me firmly. "You reach and pull yourself up, and I will be right behind you. We have come way too far to not succeed now." Adele continued in an assertive tone as she looked me dead in the eye. She was truly being the bossy big sister now, but I needed that little push. I sucked in a deep breath,, reached, and pulled myself up. For a second I was just dangling by my fingers until I realized I really could do this, (whew mind over matter really works) but my arm muscles still burned like I don't know what. I began to swing my legs back and forth to get the momentum I needed to propel my right leg up. I swung my leg to the window ledge, but I missed and nearly lost my grip with my hands.

"Evelyn!" They all screamed below.

"Please don't fall; please don't fall." I heard Gwen chanting below. I glanced down and saw that they all were holding hands and had a look of worry and dread on their faces. Well, all except Adele. I saw in her eyes a look of pride and confidence that she always gave me when I faced great opposition and thought I would fail. That look on her face gave me the extra boost of confidence as I secured my grip and swung my leg once more up onto the ledge and made it this time.

"Yay!" They all clapped and cheered below me, but I hadn't gotten in yet. I was so tired I couldn't move, and my arms hurt. I was just resting with one leg and half my upper body on the ledge taking in ragged breaths.

"Evelyn, hurry up and get the window open so you can get in." Ava called up to me. Hurry Up! Didn't she realize that my arms felt like spaghetti right about now?

"Alright, alright!" I yelled down. I reached to push the window up, hoping it wasn't locked, but no such luck. I was already breaking and entering, I didn't want destruction of property too. Oh, I forgot we already did that at the ski lodge. Well, in for a penny in for a pound. I took the rock I had put in my pocket and smashed the window near the lock above the screen. The sound was deafening in the silence of the night. I reached in, unlocked the window, pushed it up and brushed the glass off the sill before pulling myself up the rest of the way and swinging my legs in, sliding down the wall. Being careful to avoid the glass, I looked out the window planning to tell Adele to come up, but being nearly scared out of my skin, I stumbled backwards. When I looked out, she was already at the window swinging her leg up.

"Who are you? Spiderman?!" I asked her in astonishment. She swung her leg over, coming inside while grinning at me.

"I, little sister, lift weights as well. Perhaps you should start doing the same." Adele said smugly.

"Oh shut up!" I replied as I turned to leave the room.

"Adele, find the bleach container or containers while I go find a trash bag to put them in. We have to hurry." I said all this while flipping on lights as I ran down the hall to the stairs, trying to get the layout of the cabin.

"Oh my God!" Adele screamed. "Jackie did all of this!" There were bleach stains all over the place. She didn't just bleach their clothes; she bleached the furniture as well. I stopped at her words to look around and actually observe my surroundings. I saw what Adele was seeing and I was struck with shock as well. The curtains, the rugs, everything! I had never seen anything like it. I couldn't believe Jackie was capable of anything like this. Jackie hadn't just cut up clothes either; the sofas and chairs all had slices going through them.

"I swear, when we get back home I'm making Jackie see a therapist; she has lost it." Adele said in disgust as she surveyed the room. "Go on and get the trash bags. I still need to find the containers." She told me as I continued down the stairs into the kitchen. Surprisingly, Jackie had not committed any damage in this room. I found the trash bags under the sink. I decided to search the rooms on that level in the event there were any discarded bleach containers to be found. I searched room by room. There was definite evidence that Jackie had been in each and every room. Where once there were nice color schemes now showed an interruption of white where the bleach had touched it. Adele was right; our sweet Jackie had lost it!

Suddenly, my phone vibrated and it shocked me so badly my heart seemed to be pounding outside of my chest. I had zipped the phone into my inside pocket afraid that I might lose it, but I had forgotten about it throughout the night. I looked at my screen and saw that it was Sheila.

"Sheila, we're coming, we just…" She interrupted me in hysterics.

"The police are on their way up there!" She screamed.

"What?" I answered in a panic.

"They are on their way; you should be seeing the lights in a second. They just passed us." As she was saying this I looked out the window and saw them on the road. I was starting to panic.

"Sheila, I have to go. Wait for my call." I said hanging up and running upstairs to find Adele. I ran into Adele in the hallway carrying two empty bleach containers that looked to be two gallons each and a pair of scissors. Why in the world would anyone staying in a cabin in Tennessee need so much bleach? I wondered, but that was a thought left for later. She must have seen my face before I had a chance to say anything.

"What's wrong?" She asked stopping as she saw me running.

"The police are coming up the drive."

"What!!!" Adele screamed so loudly that the police could probably hear us from down the road. Put those in the trash bags while I go tell the others about the police. I dropped the bag and ran to the room where we had come in. I looked out to yell but I didn't see them and I started to panic even more. By this time, Adele had joined me and when I turned to her, tears were streaming down her face. "They're being arrested!"

Chapter Nineteen

Now this is worth crying about! "What did you say?" I was sure I had not heard her correctly. This was our worst fear come true. I looked out the bedroom in the front of the house. There were two policemen and one had a gun out on them. Adele's crying started to become harder with gulping sobs. I couldn't let myself cry; if I did I wouldn't be able to stop.

"Adele, stop crying!" I snapped at her so harshly she instantly stopped. I wasn't upset with her. I just needed her to snap out of it right away. "Listen, we have got to get out of here. You know they are going to search the house. There must be some type of silent alarm that we triggered, and they will have to check it out. They're not going to stop with just arresting them. You know this; just think about it." I could see every emotion on Adele's face and that told me just how upset she was because she was a master at masking her emotions, so showing them meant she was not in any control and she would lose it if I didn't get a handle of this situation. I saw when the full brunt of our situation and the fact that we were in jeopardy of being caught and arrested as well.

"How are we going to get out of here then?" she asked me beginning to pace.

"I don't know. Let me think." We went back to the other bedroom in the front of the house to see what was going on, thanking all that was holy that we never turned on this light. There was little to no backlight from that end of the hallway. What we saw made my stomachs muscles tighten. The only good news was that the police no longer held any guns on my family. The voice of one of the police was elevated but we couldn't hear what was being said but I could just imagine them asking, and then accusing when none of them had any I.D on them. That obviously said guilt of some kind. At least we had the forethought to leave all identification behind. They hadn't put them in the car yet but I knew they soon would. They were out in the middle of nowhere with no apparent mode of transportation and then once the police were inside they would find the destruction and break in, and then Adele and me.

What were we going to do? The solution finally came to me. "Adele, come on, we're getting out of here," I said as I grabbed her hand and led her to a different bedroom in the back of the house, but not the one we came in through.

"How?" She asked as I pulled her along.

"We're going to get on the roof," I told her.

"The roof!!!" She stopped suddenly when I said this.

"Don't stop. Keep moving," I told her giving her a little shove.

"Oh," She said and started moving again. "But why are we going in a different bedroom from the one we came through?"

"Because we're going to upset the snow on the roof and I don't want them to think we are up there. They will definitely look around the broken window; hopefully, they won't look at another window. Now come on."

We went to the furthest window away from the window we came in while still remaining away from the police in the front.

The window slid open easily; I leaned out and surveyed the roof and gutters. They didn't seem to be any higher than what we already climbed.

"Adele, you're better and faster at climbing than me, so you go first. Once you are up, I will hand you the trash bag and then you pull me up."

"Okay," She said, already climbing out to the window ledge. I just hope and pray the gutters will hold! I thought to myself.

When Adele latched on to the gutter, it screeched and we immediately stilled but I knew instantly that stopping was the wrong thing to do.

"Adele, just hurry; we either make it to the top or get caught," I told her. Apparently, I needed to say nothing more. The next thing I saw was Adele's legs, then her booted feet disappearing as she climbed up to the roof.

"I'm up. Pass me the garbage bag," She called down to me. I immediately stood up on the ledge to give her the bag. She was lying on her stomach while she hung her arms down to grab the trash bag from me. Now it was my turn. I needed to stand on the ledge then close the window before I could climb up. I put one leg out the window over the sill only now realizing that I had to stand up on the ledge in order to close the window. I was no longer just standing on a garbage can but was two stories up. I thought I was scared before, but that was nothing compared to what I was now feeling. I managed to get outside on the ledge and stand, but how I was going to close the window and hold on, I didn't know. I looked up and saw Adele staring worriedly down at me.

"I don't know how I'm going to close the window and hold on at the same time," I told her, my fear palpable, my voice trembling. Just the thought of falling to my death, knowing what that would do to Tony and the rest of my family made me want to cry. I wanted to give up and get arrested along with my sisters. Our family is full of attorneys; we would get out of it or have to do an ungodly amount of community service along with hefty fines and fees. We have the money; we would just have to live this down. Mama and Daddy may not die from the shock and fall from grace in their old age. I knew I was feeling sorry for myself, which actually didn't feel so bad. The bad part was that I was feeling sorry for myself while standing outside of a window two stories up in the freezing cold while one sister was dangling off a roof and two others were being arrested in the front of the cabin.

Getting arrested while standing outside of a window! The thought of that knocked me out of my self-induced funk right away. No one would get a picture of me in a newspaper like that. I may end up getting arrested, but I would not go down in such a humiliated fashion. Evelyn Lee Emerson is not a criminal! I thought better of that considering where I was at and what I had just been doing. Well, I was not a criminal normally!

"Evelyn, are you okay?" Adele said down to me in a hushed tone. The wind had picked up and I could barely hear her over the noise it made. I looked up at her again but I couldn't speak. "You have to hurry and get up here." I nodded my head. I had thought of a way to shut the window; I was just unsure it would work, especially now that the wind had picked up so much.

I lifted my left leg to put my foot against the window to nudge it down with my boot, but I hit it really hard, too hard. I was afraid I was about to break it each time I tried to get a grip with my boot and push it down. I finally was able to get a decent grip, and the window began to close but very slowly. I looked towards the side of the cabin and saw a flashlight beam sweeping and my blood froze. Adele saw it too. I saw it in her eyes when she looked back to me.

"Evelyn hurry!"

"I'm trying; I promise I'm moving as fast as I can." My heart was again beating so hard I was in pain. I almost had the window closed but it was slow going.

"Got it!" I said, relieved as I was finally able to get the window completely shut with my booted foot. I reached up; Adele and I locked hands. She sucked in a deep breath and she pulled as I used my feet to hoist up. As soon as I made it onto the roof on top of Adele, we saw the police round the corner. We just made it!

Chapter Twenty

As we lay on top of the roof, I thought I was smashing the life out of Adele. I was thin but so was she. I wasn't sure how long she could endure my weight, but we couldn't take a chance and move for fear we would be heard in the quiet night. We could see the flashing lights from the police car below in the front of the cabin and we could still see the beam of the flashlight moving around from an office on our side beneath us. We remained unmoving; we heard Ava in an elevated voice obviously in response to a question of what is her name asked because her response was Jeanine Woods. Adele and I looked at one another; we knew that name or rather we knew those names but not together. What was Ava doing? Jeanine was her middle name and Woods was our mother's maiden name. That was something to think about later. Apparently taking her cue from Ava we heard Gwen give her name as Renee Woods, which was her middle name and our mother's maiden again. Then we heard Anne say, "Betty Rubble."

Adele and I looked at each other again and mouthed "*The Flintstones!*" What in the world was Anne thinking, giving the name of a famous cartoon character as her name? I couldn't figure out why they were questioning them out in the freezing cold instead of just taking them back to the station. Adele and I were freezing as well, lying out on the roof. Adele most likely wasn't as cold and I since I was still lying on top of her, so my body was essentially helping to shield hers from the wind. After about fifteen long, painfully freezing minutes, we finally heard the police car drive off with our loved ones handcuffed in the back seat. We had overheard Ava and Evelyn protesting being handcuffed when there was nowhere to run off to. Anne being the wounded one was allowed to go handcuff free. I was able to roll off of Adele and let her breathe.

"What are we going to do?" Adele asked me.

"I wish I knew, but Sheila will pick us up as soon as the police car passes them and is out of sight."

"We need to get down. I would like to go through the house but we're going to have to go back the way we came just in case the alarm resets itself after a certain amount of time." We still lay on our backs on the roof trying to catch our breath as our adrenaline rush came down causing us to shiver from the cold. I was extra cold because I was wet with sweat from our extracurricular activities. Adele probably was as well. We saw an SUV come up the drive and waited until we could see their white coats that matched ours through the windows to be sure it was them, but really who else would be out here at three in the morning in the freezing cold!

I sat up, starting to make my descent down the building when Adele grabbed my arm to stop me.

"Oh my God!" She screamed as she pointed. I turned to see what she was pointing at and I started screaming as well. There was a bear right behind where Sheila had parked the car. I fumbled to get my phone out of the inside pocket of my coat. I had gotten hold of the phone, but I was shaking so badly with fear I couldn't finger my code to unlock my phone. Thank God Sheila decided to call me at that very moment because I don't think I would have ever gotten the phone unlocked to be able to dial. I answered on the first ring.

"We're here out in the front," I heard Sheila say but I couldn't seem to talk. Adele, not quite in the predicament I was in, started yelling.

"Sheila, there is a bear behind you." Sheila must have had the phone on speaker because we could suddenly hear screams from everyone in the SUV. I guess Sheila's flight response kicked in out of fear, because the SUV took off and smashed into a tree.

"Oh Lord!" I said. What if we are now stuck from her hitting that tree, but apparently that tree was no match for our monster SUV. Sheila had stopped and backed up right after she hit it and it never stalled. There didn't seem to be much damage that we could see from on top the roof.

"Sheila," I called through the phone. Apparently my vocal chords had returned. "Are you alright?"

"Yes, we're fine." She answered shakily. I could hear the fear in her voice.

"What about the bear?" Katherine asked screeching with fear. We could still see the bear. It ran from when the truck hit the tree, it seemed to be coming back, curious I supposed.

"We have to figure out how to get it away so that we can get down and leave." I said this out loud, but I was actually thinking to myself. We heard Jackie with a pained voice tell Sheila to crack the windows and turn the radio on as loud as it could go. Sheila and Katherine were arguing with her that she was crazy and that the bear would get in and eat them, but she gave such a stern and in charge voice that we had never heard Jackie make, that she said to do it and soon after we heard the blaring stereo from the SUV.

Sheila also began revving the engine and we watched as the bear ran away back into the woods.

I yelled into the phone for Sheila to drive around the back to come get us. Apparently she could not hear me over the loud music because she continued to sit in the same spot, so I texted her. We waited a moment and soon the SUV started moving in our direction to the back of the cabin but she did not turn the music down. I didn't blame her.

I've heard more people die descending a mountain than ascending one, and at that moment I could believe it because though we were not on a mountain, coming down the side of a building felt a lot higher coming down than climbing up. Once we made it down my legs felt like jelly and we just held one another tight for a few moments to steady ourselves.

"Adele, let's go." We hurriedly got in and locked the doors. "Sheila step on it!" I said. Sheila stepped on it alright;, she stomped on the gas so hard the engine revved and the tires spun and squealed before jumping forward and we all screamed in fright.

"Aaah! Sheila don't kill us!" Adele yelled.

"Sorry!"

As we drove off, I wondered why a bear had come so close to the property. I turned and looked and saw that there was an overturned garbage can with food on the ground. How had that happened? I wondered. I knew we had not turned over any trash and the cans had bear protection lids on them. As I pondered over how close we had come to being bear chow, I turned my attention back to everyone else. That was a mistake!

I thought I was stressed beyond belief already, but of course that was before I encountered everyone's worried faces in the SUV asking me what we were going to do with their eyes. But that would not do for my Jackie, who was again crying hysterically. I was barely holding it together myself so I wasn't sure I could handle her on top of everything else.

"Evelyn, they arrested them and it's all my fault and we almost were eaten by a bear!" Jackie said, crying so hard I thought she would hyperventilate.

"Jackie, calm down and breathe!" Adele told her while holding her tight in her arms. She actually was trying to obey, but she wouldn't take her eyes off me. She wanted me to hold her not Adele; Adele was the tough one that never seemed to make mistakes and pointed yours out in extreme detail She would make mincemeat of someone in court or with a legal document, not the comforting one to lean on for emotional support. This catastrophe of a vacation was bringing out the best and the worst in all of us. Jackie's breathing was finally calming down as Adele rocked her slowly. I guess Adele was over being mad with her too!

"Sheila, head back to the lodge so we can find out where that police station is located." I told her. It's too dark to go wandering around trying to find it."

"The police station? We're going there? What are we going to do?" Sheila asked in excited, rapid succession.

"I don't know." I answered her quietly. "I just don't know!"

Chapter Twenty One

We finally make it back to the lodge and I sent Katherine in to get the address and direction to the local police station. We were surprised that there was still a police car and two policemen in the parking lot seemingly still working on the car break-ins and the actual break in of the security office. I wanted to stay away just in case Kevin the bartender saw me and wanted to chat me up. I didn't want them to take the chance of our faces being seen just in case the officers here saw Ava and Gwen when they were arrested. We looked so much alike, we might get arrested on sight. Guilt by lookalike! We really didn't have the time and I definitely didn't have the energy.

"I got it!" Katherine said to us as she returned to the car from getting the address and directions of the police station. She handed the directions to Sheila who was still our designated driver. Sheila glanced over it then handed it back to Katherine in the passenger seat.

"Katherine, read the directions out to me please. That will be easier for me," Sheila told Katherine.

"Has anyone figured out what we're going to do?" Jackie asked, straining in pain as she spoke. She was in so much pain it was hard to look at her. I had to get her to a hospital but first I had to figure out how to spring them from jail.

"Not yet sweetheart." I answered her. "How's your hand?"

"It's not too bad." She lied. She was holding her entire arm inside her coat.

"Let me see it!" She didn't want to show me, but not because she didn't want me to see it; I knew she didn't want to move it because of the pain.

"It hurts too badly; I don't want to move it."

"Well, just let me open your coat so I can see it. You need to move your good arm for me." She didn't want to move and I knew nothing medically, but I still wanted to see it. She moved her uninjured arm and I moved aside her coat front. When I saw the one I nailed with the hammer I felt sick. It was the size of a catcher's mitt and it was fire engine red! I felt sick.

"Honey, we'll get to a hospital as soon as we can. I'm so sorry about your hand."

"It's not your fault; no one would be here if it weren't for me and my insane illogical actions." I had never seen Jackie look so sad except when she told us she believed Michael was cheating on her. I had not forgotten about that issue but I didn't want to bring it up and add to her distress. As we approached a small lone building up on a hill there was a pretty big sign that read Deer Oak Sheriff so I guessed we had made it. The sign was as big as the building! It was a nondescript wood building: rectangle in shape, painted brown with white trim. There was an oversized doorway for the entrance; it looked plain but well taken care of.

"Well Evelyn, what should we do now?" Sheila asked interrupting my thoughts as she slowed our ascent up the hill to the station. I really didn't know but I couldn't give up now.

"Sheila, go ahead and take us up to the station and park. Sheila started driving as I continued to give instruction. Katherine, once we get there, we need you to go in and see what's going on. Look and see how secure it is and how many officers are in there. Just get the lay of the land. There is only one other patrol car out here so I'm hoping that's all they have, but you never know. If you see the girls, act as if you don't know them. Tell the officers you're lost and need directions down to the city. Then come back out and we'll drive away and figure out our next step."

We had made it to the sheriff's station and Sheila had parked but Katherine had not made a move or a sound at this point and we all seemed to realize it at the same time as we turned in unison to stare at her.

"Well, go!" I told her when she made no move to open the door.

"Why me? Why can't you do it?" I thought I really liked my sister-in-law up to now, I really did. I know I had bullied her earlier at the chalet, but I honestly had thought nothing of it; of what I did or her response. But now, steam was about to come out of my ears. All she had done was come along for the ride. This was all for one and one for all! As I worked to clamp down my temper I was glad that I had glanced at Adele first. I thought I was mad, but compared to the look on Adele's face I knew the lawyer tongue was about to come out and pimp slap Katherine with it. She was going to say something so mean and hurtful that not only would she hurt Katherine but also our brother Duncan to whom she was married. Duncan and Adele were thick as thieves, but he would feel betrayed because it was his wife so there was no way I would allow her emotions to take over once more tonight and take the chance of damaging that relationship. I clamped down on Adele's hand

and shook it letting her know I would handle it, at the same time responding to Katherine.

"Katherine, I can't go and Adele can't go because if Ava and Gwen are in there they will know we are with them because we all look alike and you also need to go because it's your turn. So go!" I instructed her and emphasized by leaning over her and opening her door.

"Just go in and get the lay of the land. We'll be right here waiting." Katherine reluctantly got out of the SUV and slammed the door. "Well, we know how she feels, don't we!" I said in exasperation."

"She'll get over it, once this night is over and we're all safe." Sheila said from the front seat.

"Yeah, I guess you're right, we all know how she is. I shouldn't have gotten so upset," Adele said. This is why I did not let Adele's serpent tongue loose, she was already feeling bad for the amount of anger she showed towards Katherine. Adele was mean but nice at the same time!

All of a sudden Katherine was back, but way sooner than I expected. She didn't get in, but scared us half to death by knocking on the driver's side window. Sheila was so startled that it took her a few moments to find the window release to roll it down. Sheila finally found the release, but Katherine screeched.

"Come *inside now!*" before the window had barely moved an inch.

"Why? What's wrong?" I demanded fearing the unknown that I truly was not prepared for at all. Even my unknown plan was being botched before I could make it. Katherine had a look of panic on her face.

"He already knew who I was, says he's been waiting on me." Oh no, no, no! My mind was racing with the possibilities of what did he know and how did he know. Of course I knew the obvious answers were Ava, Gwendolyn or Anne had said something. If they did, I couldn't blame them; I'm sure they were terrified. Until this crazy night, none of us had ever broken the law. No, we couldn't start with shoplifting candy or something, we couldn't even go into it with both feet, we had to immerse our entire bodies into multiple felonies of breaking and entering, destruction of multiple, multiple, multiple properties. I turned to Adele and I saw her putting her emotional armor on that she used every time before stepping into a courtroom.

"You ready?" Adele asked me. Noooo, my brain was screaming but I had to regardless of how I felt so I had to get it together before stepping out of this truck. I closed my eyes, took in a deep breath and said a silent prayer and I knew I could do this. What I was about to do I did not know, but I knew I could do it. I opened my eyes looked at Adele and said, "Let's go!"

Chapter Twenty Two

We had Jackie and Sheila stay in the SUV watching us with a look of terror on their faces as we walked up to the station. Right before we got to the door Adele stopped us to give us what she obviously thought was a pep talk to bolster strength.

"Evelyn, Katherine, remember we are "*The Isaacs*"." Then she turned, opened the door and strolled in, we quickly followed. I wanted to ask her how was remembering we were the Isaacs supposed to help in this situation because I just didn't get the pep talk on that one. Being Isaacs was one of the main reasons we were in this situation; protecting our Isaacs name was everything to Adele. Obviously the pep talk did the job for her because Adele strolled in, back in form as if she owned the place.

Walking into the office I was struck stupid by what I was looking at. I know this was the resort's own little sheriff's office but we were in the year 2014; this was just a big room that strongly resembled the Mayberry jail from The Andy Griffith Show. I know I had joked earlier wondering could they be Mayberry but I never actually thought it to be true. There were three old wooden desks with the old pull- out drawers. There were two doors on opposite walls leading somewhere, I'm guessing to the bathroom and maybe another exit. There was an actual jail with real *bars*; there was also an actual hook with skeleton keys on them on the far wall across from the jail cells. I expected to see Otis lying on a cot but instead it held Ava, Anne and Gwendolyn sitting on a long bench seat. I thought they would look scared or even sad but they looked mad. Anne was obviously still in pain from whacking her head on the tree and her head was the size of a grapefruit but you could still see the anger through the pain.

The barren antiquated office must have thrown Adele off too because she was about to speak as soon as we entered but then she caught site of the place and stumbled her speech. She recovered quickly, but before she could get out more than "I'm" to introduce herself, the deputy interrupted her.

"Oh I knowed who you were the secont you walked in the door." He spoke with one of the strongest twangs I had ever heard; he had to be from somewhere from the hills of Tennessee rather than the city. "You looked just like them two we hauled in a lilt whilt ago." He continued. "Yep caught all three at the scene of de crime. So I knowed who ever was wit em would come strollin in after a whilt. Did ya get my gift?" The deputy looked very happy with himself, and he had stopped talking obviously waiting for our turn to see what we would say. I had no idea what he was talking about it.

"Gift?" I asked.

"Yous knows! I undone that trash can. It's lotsa bears ups dem mountains." Looking and sounding even more pleased with himself, grinning with brown stained teeth. We looked at one another shocked with the realization of what he had just admitted to; he tried to kill us. What kind of human being could do such a thing? I was sick with the knowledge that someone had been cruel enough to send a bear to kill us. Or hoped he would!

"Sir my name is Elizabeth Woods." Adele rebounded from being told someone intentionally tried to cause our deaths faster than I did. Adele was apparently staying with the only giving her middle name and our mother's maiden name script that we had heard Ava give them when they were arrested. "Yes, you are correct that those two ladies look like me because they are my sisters; but I have no knowledge of any crime committed. Without being able to reach them for some time, we became worried. So we came here believing the sheriff's department would help us. We walk in trying to seek assistance and not only have you arrested them for some made up crime but you accuse us as being coconspirators." Adele said indignantly but she was smooth and cool as can be. Katherine and I put on an indignant face to go along with Adele's and her righteous speech.

Deputy Douglas, which I had to read off of his uniform since he failed to introduce himself, just smiled at us. "Looka here maam," Deputy Douglas began again. "I knows I arrestet them ladies at a cabin that I knows theyed brokt into. Me and my partner was just too late to cathem in the'd act."

"Sir." I spoke up this time. However Deputy Douglas didn't let me continue either.

"Oh, you look just likem too!" Apparently he never looked me in my face before now. "Y'alls look like them dubbment twins cept it's four of ya an exceptin that one in the cage looks a bit youngern." He said pointing at Ava who was in fact the baby of the family. I just stared at him with my mouth hanging open; I didn't know what to say to that!

I tried again. "Sir." But he again interrupted me, while smiling down at me.

"Maam, I knowd you say theyed didn't do nothing but I knowd what I saw. I wishd we had better commodations for they stay tonight, but we in the middlet of a renavations and I gots no time to drivem to the court house in the city, we been too busy tonight. Wilt takem in the mornin and gettem processed. I would love to take yall in too but didn't catch y'all."

If we weren't actually guilty I would be offended; however, we still had to pretend to be offended.

"How dare you accuse me and my family of a crime?" Doing my best overly-offended act; he didn't seem to be buying it though. He just stared at us with a knowing grin that seemed to say ah ah ah, you're not getting away with this one.

"Excuse us, we need to talk privately!" I told him while hooking my arms with Katherine and Adele's pulling them with me to the other side of the room.

"Y'all go right chead, I'm here all naht!" He said while he sat down but still holding that knowing smug grin.

"Adele, what should we do?" I asked her beginning to feel like we were at the end of our rope with no more options.

"I could easily beat this if it went to court." Adele answered in a whispered tone. One problem is that if I've already told him my name was something else, I would have to go to court and give my legal name that I am licensed to practice law under so that would be a mother of red flags. The biggest problem is that though he really didn't catch them doing anything nor with anything, the cabin was broken into. So when they investigate and put it together, they will know that Anne's husband was staying there and being that Anne is one of the arrestees they will definitely be found guilty and then we are back at square one that started us on this nightmare. The only positive I see is that they have no way of linking us to the break in at the resort. Thank goodness for small favors. If we didn't care about this getting out I would gladly see them in court."

As Adele had told us this her voice became an excited whisper. Katherine looked as desolate as I felt but Adele was glowing at the prospect of arguing the case in court. Go figure!

"Gwendolyn and Ava both are lawyers; why haven't they said anything in their own defense?" Katherine asked. "They're just sitting over there looking mad enough to bite nails." Where was Katherine's mind tonight? I wondered in exasperation. Had she not been a member of our family full of lawyers for over thirty years including my brother who was her husband? But I refused to open my mouth; I just mentally shook my head at her.

"Because," Adele responded with the tone of exasperation that I felt, "they are doing exactly what they have been taught all their life to do. Say nothing and wait for your attorney! In normal circumstances that would be me but we are in nothing close to normal circumstances. At this moment I can't act as their attorney so we have to think of something else."

"Uh excuse me, ladies!" Deputy Douglas spoke to us from across the room.

"Yes." I said to him as we each turned to him to give him our full attention.

"I reckon that I maight be able to help y'all; since they ain't been no fingerprintin or paperwork done yet I'm willin to let them three dere go for a price." He said to us while still giving us that grin.

"Excuse me!" I asked in outrage.

"What?!!!" Adele exclaimed in what seemed greater outrage, at the same time Gwendolyn, Ava and Anne had jumped up from the cell bench and were also spouting out their ire through the bars.

"You are trying to extort money out of us!" I didn't know if I was asking him or just stating a fact at him. I was so upset I could barely see straight.

"Simmer down, simmer down now." Deputy Douglas said with a tone that said *"women get upset for nothing"*. This man obviously had no respect for us or possibly women in general. Looka here I knowed you ladies gots lots a money, y'all fancy matchin coats and leather gloves, boots and hats. Y'alls don't fool me none. I knowds ya did the break-in and I knowds ya got plentya money."

"Listen Deputy." I said moving to stand in front of him, but I immediately felt a hand on my arm and I stopped walking. Katherine stepped in front of me, that shocked me and I'm pretty sure I wasn't the only one because Katherine has never stepped up to center stage voluntarily. And I mean not ever!

"Sir, how much money do you want?" Katherine asked this of Deputy Douglas in a quiet voice.

"What!!!" We all screamed.

"We are not paying him any money!" I shouted. "What are you doing letting *this* man think he can blackmail us Katherine?" I said in the most offensive voice I could come up with trying to show my feelings of disgust at Deputy Douglas while I stared daggers at him. The jerk! I was breathing so hard I thought I would explode.

"We need to get them out of jail and it's obvious this man has no respect for us or the law despite the uniform he's wearing." Katherine said to me, but stared the deputy directly in the eye. "I think we need to hear what he has to say."

"Ny see, that lady gotz a lot of sense." Deputy Douglas spoke up. The shyster was really grinning now! I wanted to knock that grin off his face but I had forgotten that Daddy had taught us to always listen to what the opposition had to say and then come back with something better and crush them. Daddy meant legally and obviously Katherine *had* learned a thing or two from my brother over the years.

Katherine was right; I lifted my hand to quiet everyone down.

"Youz must be the ring leader of this here bunch!" Deputy Douglas said to me; that grin was really starting to get under my skin.

"I am not the ring of anything, deputy; but you now have our attention, so speak up." Even though he was taller than I, I knew how to look down at a person and I was definitely picturing smashing him with my booted foot and maybe a kick for good measure as well.

"Wells like I said, I knowds you all gots money. Y'alls sophisticated lookin and talks all proper and updty and your fancy coats and boots. Soes, I figurned five thousand biguns for all three each of em." Apparently none of us knew what to say because the room was silent; we could easily afford that sum of money but it was now three in the morning and we had no way to access that kind of money at that time of night, or day. I didn't know what to make of *this!* All I knew is that I was exhausted and having some podunk deputy extort money from me was more than I could handle.

"Will you accept a credit card or a check?" Katherine asked Deputy Douglas.

"Maam, do I look lika bank or credit card machine?" The deputy asked sarcastically. Katherine's eye immediately began to water.

"Im tryin' ta be nice but you's get that muney here by sevun in the mornin befores the deputies come in ta change shifs or they gets taken in to be processed."

"Ya gets that money, and I just tell em ya escaped, taint no paperwork so dey don't exists."

"Let me handle this." I told Katherine and looked back at the others giving them the look of confidence that said I got this, but I definitely wasn't feeling it. "It is three in the morning; where are we supposed to get that kind of money at this hour?" I insisted.

"That's not my problem. But ya gets it or dey stay behinz them dere bars. Ya got that?" He bent and yelled in my face. I was so startled I jumped back, in fact we all did. And his breath smelled so bad I thought I would pass out.

"How dare you scream in my sister's face?" Ava yelled but they were all screaming at him by this time. I was so insulted, I was not accustomed to being treated in such a manner. He had no idea who he was messing with.

"Calm down everyone." I shushed them trying to gain control of the room once more, but they were outraged and on a roll of screaming and yelling.

"Calm down!" I said trying to sound calm but raising my voice in a yell so I could be heard. They abruptly stopped and looked at me like I had grown another head. "It's okay, I'm alright!" I told them then I turned back to face the deputy. "I need to talk to them again privately to figure out how to get the money."

"Youz gos right chead!" His grin had wavered right before he yelled in my face and now he looked mean. The real Deputy Douglas had shown up, the fake smile now gone. I walked over to the jail cell indicating with my hand for the others to follow me.

"Evelyn, are you ok?" Gwen asked me.

"Yes, I'm fine." I assured them all as I quickly scanned the room. They didn't look like they believed me. But I finally knew what we had to do.

"We're going to have to leave…." But before I could finish my sentence, they had all taken in such a huge breath of surprise I'm sure their chest were hurting from the pressure.

"You're going to leave us?" Gwen and Ava said in unison with voices trembling and eyes wet with unshed tears as they quickly went from anger to fear. I thought my heart was breaking from the look of hurt in their eyes and the pain in my own heart that they could ever think I'd do anything like that.

I looked them all in their face.

"You didn't let me finish," I said in a soft voice. "We will be back; you know that. Even if we have to let that jerk take you in we would all go along but that's not going to happen."

"But we don't travel with that kind of cash; I only have about five hundred." Ava said crying softly.

"I know we don't have that much cash, but I'm getting you out of here." I promised as I continued to take in the details of the room. "Don't ever think that I would or could leave you in any situation, no matter what. Like Adele says, we are the Isaacs and the Isaacs stick together." I had to say this in a whisper as we all huddled together like a football team.

"You all "sit" right there on that bench; all three of you and DON'T MOVE." They each nodded their head in an affirmative. "I mean it; you "sit" right there and don't get up. We will be back before seven." I turned toward Deputy Douglas who had managed to put that fake grin along with a look of triumph on his face.

"Deputy, we need to go and get the money but we will be back before your shift change." I told him pretending that I was in agreement with him extorting money out of us.

"Sees I told ya, y'alls got the munny yas just didn't want to cough it up. Rich people nevern want to seprate from whatz they got." He went on spouting his he knows rich people speak. I assured Ava, Gwen and Anne once more that we would be back and to do what I said and to sit on that bench and not move until I returned. I knew the rest wanted to ask me what I was planning but they knew not to say anything until we were out of this place. We quickly left the sheriff's station and climbed back into the SUV. Immediately they pounced on me before I could get my seat belt fastened.

"Evelyn? What are we doing?" Adele asked.

"Where are we going to get the money at this hour?" Katherine asked. And Jackie and Sheila were both screaming what were we talking about and why hadn't the others come out with us?

"Ladies! Ladies!" I said as I held up my hand giving them the universal sign asking them to calm down and let me speak. Eventually it worked and they quieted down when they realized I hadn't responded to anything they had said to me. I realized we had yet to move and at least two minutes had passed.

"Sheila, let's go!" I snapped out. She immediately started the ignition and put the truck in gear, but looked at me cautiously before actually putting her foot on the gas. I knew she didn't understand we had to leave our sisters behind and she was scared. I saw her looking at me in the rearview mirror. "Sheila, trust me; now go and quickly please!"

Chapter Twenty Three

As Sheila drove us down the hill, I let her and Jackie in on what had happened inside the little sheriff's office and our run in with Deputy Douglas. Jackie and Sheila couldn't believe the audacity of how we were being treated by the deputy of this little resort town. If I weren't living it, I would be amazed myself.

"Well, what are we going to do? You haven't told us!" Adele said to me in exasperation as we continued down the long lonely pitch black road. "Okay," I said as I looked at my watch! It's going on four in the morning and we don't have much time but we need to hurry back to the chalet and get everything packed up. That's the first thing we need to do and fast. We need to be out of there no later than five thirty at the latest. As we are packing I will figure out what we're to do next. They all turned and looked at one another with a worried look on their face and we did have a lot to be worried about. Our troubles were yet to be over! I already had a plan worked out but I had no intention of telling them until it was too late!

After a slow, scary and very cautious drive back up the long drive to the chalet, we finally made it safe and sound. Well, as I thought more on it, we were safe. None of us were sound; not tonight anyway! We all first went to our own rooms to pack our own things as quickly as we could, then we double teamed to pack the ones who weren't with us. Except for Jackie who couldn't pack anything of her own because of her hand, Katherine had given her more pain meds and wrapped her hand in ice, now she was lying on the couch asleep in the living room. Sheila and I both packed up Jackie's things while everyone else tried to clean the chalet the best they could in under an hour.

"Evelyn?" Sheila asked me in a quiet voice. I was in the middle of zipping Jackie's numerous boots in her suitcase professionally labeled "Boots" of all things.

"Mmmh?" I answered her as I continued taking clothes out of the closet to pack. "Have you thought about what we're going to do to get them out of jail?" I could hear the fear in Sheila's voice and I couldn't blame her but I had gone from afraid to being determined.

"Yes I have." I responded to her question but never stopping or slowing in my packing of Jackie's things. "I know you are worried," I continued to explain to her. "But trust me when I say we are going to get them out and as soon as we do we are heading home. I can't tell you just yet what I have planned, but please try not to worry. That horrible and corruptible Deputy Douglas will not get the best of us regardless of what he thinks; he won't know what hit him." While I said this, I had finally stopped packing and had turned to look at her so she could see in my eyes that I meant what I was saying one hundred percent. She suddenly grabbed me and hugged me so tightly I thought she was going to crack a few ribs but I hugged her back but with less force. We all had such a long history with one another with Sheila being married to my brother Harper for close to twenty-five years and having dated him for five years before that, ever since high school. We had all cried and laughed together more times than I could count over so many years. Sheila was a wonderful sister-in-law but a great friend as well.

"I trust you." She said finally letting me go and pulled away but kissed me on the cheek before resuming her part of packing Jackie's things. Until she told me she trusted me I didn't know I needed to hear it but I had needed it; so very much.

"Ladies; are we ready?" I called out raising my voice to near yelling so I could be heard throughout the chalet. "It's almost five-thirty and we need to get the SUV's packed up."

"Yes, we're ready, and we've already begun loading." Adele yelled back from the entryway as Sheila and I were coming down the stairs pulling Jackie's numerous suitcases along.

"Did anyone wake Jackie up yet?" I asked.

"Yes, she's in the bathroom." Adele replied as Jackie herself came down the hallway towards us.

"There's the little trouble maker." I said to her, my tone was light. Jackie returned a slight smile. "Jackie, I thought Adele was bad, but you have more luggage than even her." I said while handing her the carryon and her purse which really didn't lighten my load.

"I'm sorry, but you know I can't ever decide on what I want to wear so I always bring extras." Jackie tried to explain but not really sounding sorry about it because this was her and we knew that, but we never had to carry all of her things along with our own.

With the food, we had a lot more to pack leaving than we did coming. We managed to smash and shove it all in, despite that it couldn't be packed with any kind of order for lack of time. It was already five-thirty and we had to be on our way. "Katherine, I need you to drive and everyone but Sheila ride with her in that SUV.

Sheila, I need you to drive me to the bottom of the driveway. After that, you ride with them." After I said that they all turned and looked around at one another.

"Evelyn, what are you saying? You can't go alone!" Adele asking both a question and making a statement before I could respond!

"Listen," I said trying to explain to them. "I know you all don't understand, but in the event that something goes wrong, I don't want you with me. Adele, I need you to create another distraction as you did earlier. We need to get Deputy Douglas out and away from that station. I don't believe he will be too concerned about leaving them there alone."

Sheila walked and stood in front of me and grabbed my arms. "Evelyn, I don't know what you are planning to do, but you are not going alone," She said very sternly.

"Sheila, I know you are concerned for me but…"

"No!" She shouted at me. I don't care what you say; we are not letting you go alone. This entire night we have all been in this together and that does not end, not now and not ever. I have never been more afraid than I am right now or this entire night. But you have kept everyone from going out of our minds and focused, but you need us just like we need you and you will never go alone. She was clutching my arm so tightly I was in pain. Obviously, Sheila was not having anything I was saying and she wasn't finished shouting at me either."

"I understand," she continued, finally releasing her grip on my arms, "that some of us need to go back up to the chalet, but you're not going up to that sheriff's station alone."

"Evelyn, you're not going alone." Jackie chimed in seconding the motion.

"Fine." I said, conceding that I had no choice but to take someone with me." Sheila will go with me if that's okay with her."

"Of course I'll go with you, *Idiot.*" Sheila hadn't actually called me an idiot but her tone definitely implied it.

"No, I'll go with you," Adele said.

"No Adele, I really believe you are the one to figure out how to get the attention needed without getting caught. You're a born leader and you know it and the coolest under pressure," I went on explaining. "The chalet is away from town and getting out of here you're going to have to make sure you are somewhere they can't see you. Get past them to make it back to the main road to meet us. I don't know how you're going to do that, and that worries me as well, but if anyone can do it, you can. We are going to pull in and wait in those trees down the road from the station. When we see the deputy pull out we will text you to let you know he's coming your way. We won't know where the other officers are or are coming from, but make it good to get them all there. I don't think they have more than two or three cars so that shouldn't be too difficult."

"Once you see them your way, get out of there and meet us at that boarded up old gas station we saw on our way here. That's on that side street right before we came up to the welcome to the resort sign." I had finished giving them my instructions and I felt like the weight of everyone's fate were sitting on my shoulders. I couldn't let them down.

"You're sure?" Adele asked me as she hugged me.

"Yes. Now you all get in the car and go. We have less than an hour to get this done *and* we still have to make it down this horrific hill again." Everyone could hear the fear in my voice of going down the hill again in the dead of night. It was going on six in the morning but the sky seemed to be darker than ever, instead of getting lighter in preparation of the new day. I guess it's true what they say; it's darkest before the dawn in all situations!

Sheila and I watched as Katherine and the others headed down the long dark drive, I was terrified for them and us. Soon we were heading down after them and I closed my eyes and clutched the handhold until we reached the bottom.

We followed Katherine in the first SUV until we reached the turn off that lead to the Sheriff's station and Katherine drove on down the road while we turned off.

"Sheila, pull over there!" I told her pointing to the large section of trees and bushes off to our left. "If we park there we can see when the deputy leaves and by turning the lights off they won't be able to see us."

"Okay." She said as she backed the SUV into the forest of trees and turned the lights off. "What do we do now?"

"Now we wait!" I said.

Chapter Twenty Four

While we waited, I had changed places with Sheila so I was now in the driver's seat and she was sitting in the back. I glanced at my watch again and noticed the time was quickly approaching six-thirty in the morning. "Come on Adele; we're running out of time." I murmured aloud. No sooner had I spoken the words that we saw the flashing lights of the patrol car coming down the hill from the sheriff's station and they were moving fast.

"Buckle up Sheila he's coming now." I said excitedly. I watched Sheila in the rearview mirror put on her seatbelt as I put mine on as well. "Text Katherine and Adele to let them know the deputy is on his way."

"I'm already on it!" She said, holding up the phone so I could see it in the mirror.

"Great!"

"Sheila, be ready to jump out and get that key to open the cell and make sure you are wearing your gloves."

"I'll be ready. Let's get them out of there." Sheila was so excited she was practically bouncing in her seat.

"Be careful; you're going to strangle yourself on that seatbelt if you're not careful." I told her but I really wasn't trying to stifle her excitement; I was feeling it as well. We were so close and I had hoped that things would go smoothly from this point.

The sheriff's car finally made it to the end of the street. As the car made the turn, I saw Deputy Douglas in the driver's seat tearing up the road.

"Evelyn, let's go!" Sheila screamed at me from the back seat.

"I'm going! I'm going! But he needs to be out of sight so he won't see us in his rearview mirror."

"Okay, he's gone." I said after watching him disappear up the road. I turned the lights on and floored the gas. I spun the tires and bounced us like a basketball trying to get us out of the dirt and trees. We made it. I sped up the road beyond, ready to get my sisters and go home.

We drove up to the station, and before I could get the car into park and to a complete stop, Sheila had already jumped out of the car. I guess she was more than ready to get the hell out of Dodge as well. I parked the car, but left it running, I met Sheila at the door, but we couldn't get in.

"Can you believe he locked the door?" She asked in extreme exasperation. I could, and this was actually what I had thought would happen, I had only a thread of hope that things would go smoothly from here on out and that the darn door would be unlocked. That thread was now gone!

I banged on the door calling them. "Ava! Gwen! Can you hear me? Anne!" I continued calling.

"Yes, we can hear you a little." I heard one of them call out to me, but I couldn't tell which one it was the door was so thick.

"Hold on!" I yelled back. We ran around to the left side of the building to the window closest to the jail cell.

"Can you hear me better now?" I called again.

"Yes." I heard them a lot clearer, but there was no way we would be getting through that window. It was way too small and it had bars on it as well.

"I just got Katherine's text; they are at the gas station waiting." Sheila told me, looking at her phone. "Great! Thank God something's gone right." I said.

"Evelyn, how are you going to get us out of here?" I heard Ava asked.

"Do you remember what I told you to do?" I yelled back again.

"Yes. Sit down together on the bench."

"Good, do that right now and cover your heads. I'll be there in a minute." I had enough of this night and we were getting out of here now.

"What?!!!" I heard them all scream at me. I could hear in their voices that they were scared and confused, but I didn't have time to explain.

"Just do it, now!" I yelled. "Sheila, come on." I called to her as I ran back to the SUV. Sheila and I jumped back in and I got my seatbelt buckled, put the gear in drive, and headed back down the hill.

"Evelyn, what are you doing? You said we were going in though I don't know how, and now we're leaving." Sheila said to me from the backseat near hysteria.

"I said we would be there in a minute and we are. Is your seatbelt fastened?" I called back as I slowed and made a U-turn.

"Yes but why?" Sheila responded. "Evelyn, oh my God! Are you about to do what I think you're about to do?"

"Put your head down," was my response as I floored the SUV back up the hill. I was heading for the right front corner of the building to stay as far away from injuring them as possible.

The building was getting closer and closer as I built up speed. Sheila hadn't yet put her head down as I told her. She was calling "Jesus, Jesus, Jesus" over and over again and her voice was too close to my ear. "Sheila *get down now!*" I yelled right before I crashed through the Dear Oak Sheriff's Department and threw my body down on the seat.

I had never experienced anything like it before and hopefully never will again. I had to remember to hold on to the steering wheel as I ducked down on the seat so we wouldn't crash into the actual cell, and at the same time remember to brake so we wouldn't go crashing through the back of the building. The latter was the hardest part; I was braking as hard as I could, but I had gotten pulled by the seatbelt and slammed in the shoulder by the air bag. The force of the airbag was extremely painful, but I couldn't stop to rub and try and soothe my shoulder as my first instincts kicked in to do because we were still moving and I couldn't see. We finally came to a complete stop and the airbag had deflated, but I still couldn't see. Apparently crashing through the building had knocked out the electricity and there were plumes of smoke and dust all around. Sheila had stopped screaming once we stopped.

"Sheila," I called. "Are you're still with me?"

"I think I'm dead!" She replied back still with her head down.

"You're okay," I said. I tried opening my door to get out but it was jammed shut. I moved over to the passenger door to climb out that way. I could hear Ava coughing and asking the others if they were all right.

"I'll be there in a minute; I need to get the key!" I said as I climbed over debris to the hook that held the key. I looked back and saw that Sheila had made it out behind me on wobbly legs. "Go over to them while I get the key!" I told her. Sheila looked at me and nodded in agreement but she didn't look *"all there"*.

"You okay?"

"Yeah!" She answered, still not looking *here*, but she was moving and that was all I could ask for. Time was moving regardless of how much I wanted to stop the clock. I finally reached the hook with the key, but there was no key. Oh no! My heart starting beating like a marching band's bass drums; hard and fast. Sweat popped out on my brow. I knew I was panicking, but I couldn't help it. We had come way too far to be stopped now.

What are we going to do? The tears were starting to flow down my face; I looked down and there was the key laying on the floor. Thank you Lord!

"Evelyn, do you have the key?" Gwen asked me.

"Yes, I have it." I said, starting to climb over the debris, again making my way to spring my sisters.

As soon as I opened the cell we all fell into one another crying with a mixture of joy, hope, fear and shock at what had all happened and what I had done to fix it.

"Evelyn, I can't believe you crashed through the building." Ava said crying while we held each other tight.

"I promised I was coming back and that I would get you out and I meant it! But we have to get out of here; it's almost seven. Let's go!"

As I turned around to go back to the SUV, this was the first chance I had gotten to look at the damage. I had torn the body apart in the front and the front driver's side panel which had caused the front door to jam. The body was torn apart, but amazingly it was all still attached, just mangled. I was surprised there wasn't much more damage considering what I had just put it through and the crash into the tree earlier that evening. The engine was as strong as ever and we would need the big girl to get us out of here fast.

We got back in as fast as the debris climbing would allow. Right before backing out of the building I looked at my watch and saw that it was ten minutes to seven. Once again I floored it, practically flying down the hill. As I flew down the hill I was contemplating the upcoming turn, but I knew driving as fast as I was there was no way I could make it without flipping over and killing us in the process. Then the entire night would be in vain!

"Evelyn, slow down or we'll never make the turn!" Ava who was sitting next to me screamed, but I couldn't slow down. I couldn't take the chance of us being caught. Not now! I decided to take a short cut across the uneven dirt field that ran parallel to the road. I don't know if that was a good thing or a bad thing but it was the only choice I had. I was moving ninety miles an hour and when we hit the dirt, I think we plopped in the air a good thirty feet before slamming back down.

"Aaaaahhh!" We all screamed at the top of our lungs. Our heads hit the top of the roof but I kept going as fast as I could. The dirt caused me to drop the speed to sixty. On the terrain we were traveling, fifteen or twenty would have been the safest speed, but I couldn't think about that. We had to get out of there as fast as possible at any cost but death.

"Somebody, call Adele and tell her we won't be stopping and to pull out to the corner and wait. Tell her we'll be moving fast and to follow us out." I called out. I glanced at them in the back seat and saw their bodies just bouncing up and down as we hit dirt mound after dirt mound. We should have been riding quads for this, but all we had was a luxury SUV.

I heard Adele screaming through the phone asking us where we were. "We're on our way if Evelyn doesn't kill us first." Sheila responded to her on the phone. I rolled my eyes while I listened to her tell Adele we would be there in about a minute.

I finally got us out of the dirt and I heard a collective sigh of relief from everyone including myself. I managed not to swerve too much getting us back on the road, but since I had come down at a diagonal, we were on the road we needed to turn on without having to actually make the turn.

"Sheila, do you still have Adele on the phone?" I asked.

"Yes!" She replied.

"Tell her we are about to pass her in a few seconds." Before I finished my sentence I saw I was passing her, back up at my ninety miles per hour.

I heard them all scream through the phone for me to slow down as Katherine tried to catch up with me, but they didn't know yet what I had done and knowing the sheriff would be after us once they saw the damage and that we were gone. We were still in their town! It was now getting very bright; I wasn't taking any chances.

I drove without stopping until we needed gas; there we also put the license plates back on the SUVS. I had even drove on the Tennessee highway, much slower of course, but refusing to let my fear stop me from getting as far to safety as possible. I didn't stop until we crossed the sign that said Welcome to Kentucky the Birthplace of Abraham Lincoln.

Chapter Twenty Five

We were now in the waiting room of a local Kentucky hospital emergency department. All hospital waiting rooms seem to look basically the same; rows of uncomfortable chairs, white walls, partitions to separate the admissions and registration people, and extremely bright lighting. We had been waiting two hours for Jackie and Anne to be seen and we were exhausted. While we waited, I finally told the others what had happened at the sheriff's station. Surprisingly, they were worried about my emotional state. "Evelyn, are you sure you're okay after having done something like that?" Katherine asked me.

"You sure you don't need to see a doctor with us?" Jackie asked.

"And what would I tell them I needed to see them for; crashing through a building to break my sisters out of jail? I'm fine; I'm not hurt, just a little bruised, which is expected. I just wish they would hurry up so we can leave." They didn't look like they believed me.

"Look," I said. "We've all been through the same things tonight, and except for needing some minor patch work, we're all fine."

Jackie and Anne's names were suddenly called, which took us by surprise since we had no idea people could be called simultaneously. However, waiting unreasonably long times seemed to be the norm regardless of what hospital and state you happened to be in.

I was so tired I thought I would collapse at any moment, but there was nothing to do but wait. I'm sure they felt the same. We hadn't slept in close to twenty four hours and we looked like it too. We looked like a bedraggled site, our once pristine white snow suits that were purchased for the caper were now smudged and dirty and looked more grey than white. The perfectly applied makeup we wore every day had long ago worn off. Now we wore sunken and dark eyes from lack of sleep, our faces smudged and dirty, and we had a head and hand injury to go along with everything else. If they didn't finish with Jackie and Anne soon I was going to be lying out on the floor asleep.

After another hour and a half, Anne came out but no Jackie. I suppose getting called at the same time did not equal getting released at the same time. Anne's head was wrapped up and she looked pretty decent; exhausted like the rest of us but decent, considering.

"Anne, what did the doctor say?" Gwen asked. Adele, Katherine and Sheila had managed to nod off in the uncomfortable waiting room chairs.

"I only have a minor concussion and surface injuries but nothing more." She explained as she sat in her seat across from me.

"That's good; hopefully they will be finished with Jackie soon." Gwen said. "We need to get some food and sleep."

"Anne, did they give you your bill?" I asked her.

"Yes. I will have to send them payments once I get back home."

"Give me the bill!"

"What? Oh no Evelyn, I couldn't. It's really high and you've done more than enough for me already. I couldn't ask you to do anything else." Anne said to me in clear distress.

"Anne, I will pay the bill today, and Gwen or Adele will be handling your divorce. When you start getting alimony you can pay me back." She looked like she was about to cry. Good Lord, I thought, I couldn't handle anymore tears and might lose my temper if she did. I realized I was extremely irritable, I needed rest.

"I can't believe you're still willing to help me with anything; not after everything I've caused."

"Anne, you weren't the cause of anything; you and I both know that was Jackie!" I told her in complete sincerity. "Now, please say nothing else about the money!"

"Alright! Thank you!" She told me.

I nodded my head at her, letting her know she was welcome. Ava was sitting right next to me awake, but she had said nothing the entire time. This surprised me and I told her so.

"I'm too tired to talk, so stop talking to me so I won't have to respond." That was all Ava was willing to say.

Jackie finally was released close to two in the afternoon; she was wearing a cast over her hand and up her arm, halfway to her elbow with only her fingers free. She still looked to be in a lot of pain but at least we could now leave to find somewhere to get something to eat and sleep.

"What took so long?" Gwen asked Jackie as soon as we saw her walking towards us.

"I don't know. They were just slow. They did an x-ray; then I waited and waited. Then they drained the fluid because it had swelled again. Then more waiting. Finally, they put the cast on. Then I waited some more for them to release me. They gave me my bill and now I'm here talking to you. Did you think I went off to a party or something?" Jackie responded irritably. "I'm tired too." Gwen just stared at her!

After paying the bills we drove around until we found a Waffle Kitchen so we could eat. We would have preferred a more fine dining experience since we didn't care for diners but we were way too hungry, dirty and tired to be picky or choosy.

We quickly found two booths in the back to accommodate our group; a tall redheaded woman with pale skin in a waitress uniform came up to our tables.

"Hello ladies, I'm Mandy. I'll be your waitress today." Mandy's southern accent was much different than *that* Deputy Douglas'; Mandy's was nice and somewhat musical in quality. However, she popped gum like Florence Jean Castleberry from the show Alice. Chewing gum was a nasty habit and popping gum made it even worse.

"Hello!" We all said back to her like good, tired students. We managed to order our food and be fed well; we ate as if it were our last meal on earth as well the best meal we'd ever had. I don't think we had ever eaten so much in our lives at one time. I know I hadn't anyway! We barely slowed down long enough to help Jackie who needed help cutting her food.

I signaled the waitress Mandy for our check; we were more than ready for some sleep.

"How was your ladies' lunch?" Mandy asked us.

"It was just fine, as you can see." I said waiving my hand towards all of our empty plates. "We practically licked our plates clean."

"You ladies looked wiped out, if you don't mind me saying so!"

"No, it's fine, and yes, we are indeed. Can you tell us where we may find a hotel?"

"Well, there's a real nice hotel about ten miles north of here. It's called the Royal Blue Grass Gardens. I had my wedding reception there. That's been some years ago now, but it's still really nice." She told us as she handed me the check.

"Well, thank you Mandy, I think that's where we'll go." I paid the bill and gave Mandy a generous tip for our group. If only she worked in a much nicer place; she was great waitress.

We managed to find the Royal Blue Grass Gardens Hotel, and it was a pretty nice hotel, Mandy chose a nice place for her reception. Thankfully, we were in the middle of the winter and there were plenty of rooms available, so we all were able to get our own.

Once I got to my room I took a long hot shower then threw myself into bed, my last thoughts before I fell into my coma-like sleep was how much I wished I were home with my husband; I slept for twelve straight hours.

When I awoke it was nearly six in the morning. At first I couldn't figure out what to do next. I felt like I needed a run, but at the same time I just wanted to get dressed and go home. I knew it was too early to just call everyone's rooms and say let's go. They had to be at least as tired as I was. What was I going to tell Tony about what happened? Would I tell Tony about what happened? I wasn't used to keeping things from him unless it was someone else's secret, but I was smack dab in the middle of all of it and not telling him seemed wrong. No, it didn't seem wrong it was wrong! I have never broken the law like I just had. Our family upheld and enforced the law, and to tell my own husband that his wife had turned into a mass criminal overnight, well the thought was just horrifying. I hadn't really thought about how all of this would affect Tony; I only concentrated on Jackie and my parents and that wasn't like me. Tony was my whole world now that my children had grown up and started their own lives and families. He put me first all the time and I hadn't thought of him or his career. I only gave it a passing thought. What if none of this had worked out and we were now sitting in jail? Was I a horrible, inconsiderate wife instead of the loving and supportive one I believed I was all these years?

My thoughts were running me insane; I decided I did, in fact need to go for a run. The hotel had a fitness center so I decided to brave the dreaded treadmill and try to run off some of my stress.

It didn't work! When I got to the hotel's fitness center Adele was already there in a full sweat running on one of the multiple treadmills they had. We only acknowledged one another with a slight wave of the hand. I ran fifteen miles and I was not feeling any better. I was drenched in sweat but still no less stressed. It was time to go home.

Thirty minutes later, I was in the lobby impatiently waiting. I couldn't even have the valet bring the SUVS if the women weren't there to drive them. Finally, I saw Anne and Jackie get off an elevator. I motioned to them making sure they saw me right away. "Where is everyone else?" I demanded to them once they reached me.

"They're coming; you didn't give us much time. You called and said we're leaving in thirty minutes. We haven't even had breakfast, and I need something on my stomach to take my pain meds." Jackie said whining.

"We'll stop and get something when we leave. And thirty minutes is plenty of time to get a shower and get down stairs." I said back to her. "I am ready to go. I don't…" I was interrupted by seeing the rest of them walk out of the elevator looking perfectly coifed. I should have known.

"Are you all finally ready?" I asked in extreme exaggeration showing how frustrated I was with them for dragging their feet.

"Evelyn, we are only running behind a few minutes," Gwen said back.

"I have been waiting for forty-five minutes. I said thirty. This has been the trip from hell and I'm ready to go home. Now let's go!" I immediately turned and walked outside giving the tickets to the valet attendants.

We had been back on the road for close to an hour after stopping for breakfast, but no one was talking. I realized that I was more than likely the cause of everyone's silence and my attitude was a bit over the top, but I just didn't care. They were my sisters; they'd get over it. As much as I loved them, I couldn't wait to get them home and be rid of them for a few days.

"Ava," I said. "I haven't asked you how you're feeling after all this." Ava was driving as she did on our way down, but this time I was in the front passenger seat instead of the rear and I could clearly see the stress in how her hands were clenching the steering wheel.

"Oh, I'm doing alright. I never could have imagined ever getting arrested in my entire life, none of us could."

"Yeah, I know. Me either. Or anything else we got into."

"But Ev, I'm worried about you more."

"Me, Why?"

"Because we put everything on you to figure things out, without stopping to think of how much pressure that would be on you."

"There was no more pressure on me than anyone else."

"Yes there was! Because of Jackie you felt you couldn't fail and she asked you to figure everything out and we didn't help you."

"What are you talking about?" I asked her in disbelief. "If you didn't help me you wouldn't have ended up in jail."

"True, but we didn't help you plan, and all of that must have weighed on you so much."

"It wasn't so bad." I lied. "I had you all with me and that made everything all right." I needed to assure her I was fine regardless of how I really felt; I really didn't know how I felt or how I should feel. All I knew was that I wanted to get home and possibly after that I could determine exactly what I was feeling.

Chapter Twenty Six

We finally pulled into my driveway; everyone had parked their cars on the street the morning we left so all they had to do was get their luggage and go. We had stopped about twenty minutes before to use the restroom so everyone was in as much of a hurry to leave as I wanted them to. And as much as I wanted them to leave, we had to discuss one more thing. "Hey," I said. "Everybody come over here." They all came towards me looking as tired as I felt. I could tell Katherine was still mad at me but so what!

"We tell no one what happened! I mean no one, not your husband, not your kids, no one." I told them in a firm voice.

"I will tell Tony I wrecked the truck by hitting a building which is true. He doesn't need to know I hit a building by driving through it."

We all agreed to keep our horrendous trip details to ourselves, hugged and kissed before I watched them drive away. I grabbed my large Pullman, carry on and purse and lugged it into the house. As I came through the kitchen door and headed for the back stairs, I saw Janice coming through the door from the laundry room.

"Evelyn, what are you doing home?" Janice asked, startled to see me. I didn't know what to say to her; all of a sudden I started feeling the realization and weight of what we had been through. I felt as if it were crashing down over me. I felt my eyes begin to water and a tremble in my hands; I turned away from her hoping she hadn't seen my face.

"Um, we just needed to come back early that's all." I answered her as I turned beginning my ascent up the stairs. My voice had started to tremble as my tears began to stream down my face. I couldn't face her; I needed to get to the sanctuary of my room. I tried to pick up the pace as I clamored up the stairs but my luggage was slowing me down.

"Evelyn, what's wrong?" Janice was sounding worried at my odd behavior and hearing the tears in my voice.

"Nothing, I'm just tired; I need to lie down." I lied again, still lugging my luggage; it didn't feel this heavy before. Would I ever make it up the freaking stairs?

"Evelyn, let me help you with your luggage."

"No!" I called behind me. "I got it!" I was too emotional to talk and if I stopped and even looked at her, I knew I would break down right then and there. I was already crying. I just needed to make it to my room.

"OH MY GOD, the SUV!" Janice screamed as she obviously saw the destroyed SUV out the window. By this time I had finally made it up the stairs and was practically running down the hall pulling my luggage behind me. I heard Janice running up the stairs after me but I had made it to my room and shut the door.

Behind my door the tears really started and they wouldn't stop. I heard Janice knocking on the door begging me to let her come inside but I couldn't talk to her. How could I explain that we could have been eaten by a bear and that I had driven through a police station to break my sisters out of jail? That I, Evelyn Lee

Emerson, not only born to a judge and raised to uphold the law, but the wife of a judge, had broken more laws than I could have ever imagined breaking. I was a criminal, most likely wanted by the law. The more I thought, the more I cried. I lay on my bed fully clothed; I had not even taken off my coat or boots. I just cried! I didn't know how long I had been crying but I suddenly felt strong hands pulling me into even stronger arms and a solid chest. My Tony was here!

I just hugged his neck so tight; I was never letting go. He held me on his lap as I guess what; yes cried and cried and cried.

"Evelyn, I need you to stop crying and talk to me." Tony's voice was so calm and soothing, but also worried. I held my face down in his chest, I was being scratched by the wool of his coat, but I couldn't look at him either. I couldn't bear to face and tell him what happened and see the look of disappointment that would come on his face.

"Evelyn, look at me."

"I can't!"

"What do you mean you can't? Since when do you keep things from me? He asked softly. You have me worried. What's going on?"

How could I explain to him that I wasn't really trying to keep anything from him? I had made a promise not to tell but I had to tell him something and something fast.

So I told him about Jackie and Michael, Anne and her husband and Jackie and Adele fighting and me running the truck into a building while not paying attention to what I was doing. I felt so bad for not telling him the whole truth and for allowing him to believe that was all there was, that I was sick to my soul over it. But what else could I do?

He was a judge, he didn't break the law, he enforced it; he couldn't find out his wife had broken nearly every one of them all. I was so ashamed!

He assumed I was so distraught because of all of this, but of course he didn't know the half of it. And Lord willing, he never would.

Eventually, we removed our coats and shoes and I fell asleep exhausted.

Chapter Twenty Seven

After sleeping for another ten hours then waking up to eat. I took a bath, and I again went back to sleep, I finally felt like myself the next morning.

I went out and made my morning run. I didn't care how cold it was, I needed to feel the air in my face and just knowing we were all free gave me an extra incentive to run regardless of the weather. After returning home and taking a shower, I dressed in jeans and a sweater and went down to the kitchen to face Janice.

I walked in the kitchen and Janice was at the stove frying eggs like always. When she heard me, she turned to look at me then walked over and gave me a hug. "Good morning; are you feeling better this morning?" Janice asked me before turning back to the stove.

"Yes, yes I do. I want to apologize about yesterday; I shouldn't have run away like that."

"Evelyn honey, you have nothing to be sorry about. You didn't do anything wrong. I understand you were upset and couldn't talk. That's why I called Tony. He's what you needed." She said, giving me a wink and a sly smile. I ducked my head and smiled back.

"No comment!" I said back.

"Sit down so you can eat." She ushered me with her hands to sit.

"I need to get some coffee first."

"No, you don't. I'll get it; you just sit down like I said." She always bullied me, I was pretty sure she worked for me. I thought laughing as I obeyed and sat down.

"Ok, well since I have to sit, you sit down with me; I want to tell you what happened." And I did!

Yes, I know I broke my promise to not tell despite making the others swear, but this was Janice. She is my best friend; there was no one closer except for my actual sisters, and Tony so I refuse to feel guilt about breaking my word.

"Evelyn, I can't believe what all you went through; you could have died. Why didn't you all just come home right away?" Janice was now crying; that it was all over didn't seem to matter.

"Janice, please don't cry, I can't take anymore tears." I said trying to comfort her in a soothing tone and patting her on the arm. Arm pats never did anything. I don't know why I was now trying it myself but it seemed the thing to do.

"I realize now we should have come home, but at the time we just weren't thinking like that. All we could think about was making sure Mama and Daddy never found out any of it. We were afraid it might hurt them too bad to have the reputation they've spent their entire life building torn apart in their old age. They didn't deserve that."

"I suppose you're right, but never do anything like that ever again!" She demanded.

"I promise I won't. And considering I got to this age before anything like that ever happened, I'm sure nothing else could ever come close. I'm happy to get back to my husband, home, and life."

"What about Jackie? She's never acted like this before."

"Yes I know! I don't know; I assume she's doing better. I haven't talked to her. I know she didn't want to tell Michael about all that happened, but she has to tell him something. At least about how she has begun drinking because of her suspicions of him and that Yolanda person."

"Are you still planning on going to the office to see Michael's assistant?" She asked me, very curious about the so-called sex goddess.

"Oh yes I am! I don't want to, but the way Jackie was acting, it may be all dreamed up in her mind. But, I'm not taking any chances; I'm going to find out for myself. I'm going to wait until Monday though; I don't feel like going anywhere for a while. I just plan to relax around the house."

"Good. You never relax anymore; you're always on the go or at your office." Janice was chastising me again, but I didn't say anything in my defense this time, I never seemed to win anyway.

* * * *

Our office building was fairly new; only five years old. We had managed to buy prime real estate downtown on a block that had old buildings that were practically falling down. We bought the land, torn down the building and built a new one that stood eight stories high with an underground garage. The building was all black glass and chrome, very modern in design. I always felt proud of my family when I walked in the building.

On Monday morning I felt glorious. After spending the weekend going to the spa for the works treatment that included getting my hair and nails done, I felt and looked like a million dollars. As I stepped off the elevator, I did a quick inventory of myself; I had on a gorgeous beige power suit, and matching coat, and light gold leather boots that complemented the suit perfectly. My makeup and hair were flawless. I was ready to take on Yolanda the assistant.

I walked in the lobby of his office and froze in my tracks as soon as I saw Yolanda. I knew who she was as soon as I saw her. She was standing watering the plants at the window.

Yolanda was HOT! I mean she was va va va voom HOT! She was average height and weight but top heavy and very hippy; very shapely like the old coke bottles. Her face was average with a somewhat long, thin jaw, wide set eyes and average nose size. I had to stop and reflect for a moment and remember that not only was I considered to look like the gorgeous legendary actress Dorothy Dandridge who was the prettiest black woman ever to grace the Hollywood screen, but to remember Jackie looked just like me, so she had no reason to be intimidated by Ms. Sextress, regardless of her breast size.

"Hello," I said, putting on my best smile while offering her my hand to shake. "I'm Evelyn Emerson; I'm here to see Mr. Lawrence." She shook my hand, smiling back.

"Hi. Can you tell me which Mr. Lawrence you are here to see?" She seemed nice enough, though she seemed to be dressed for going to some club instead of the front office of an accounting firm. What is Michael thinking allowing her to dress in such an unprofessional manner?

"Oh, excuse me. I'm here to see Michael Lawrence." I said, still smiling at her. I had forgotten that Michael's brother worked here as well.

"One moment please!" She said as she sat at her desk and began looking through what appeared to be an appointment book on her computer.

"I'm sorry Ms. Emerson, but I don't see that he has you scheduled." Yolanda was very proficient at her job.

"No problem. I don't need an appointment I'm his sister-in-law and I just wanted to stop by and say hello."

"Oh, you do look like Mrs. Lawrence now that I think about it," She said to me smiling, but she didn't seem to be at ease anymore and I wondered why since I hadn't done anything but tell her who I was. And how did she not recognize my resemblance to Jackie? She saw her once a week and my other sisters worked upstairs. Didn't she ever see them? Hmmm… Possibly not; let me not jump to conclusions.

"One moment, let me just call him." She said as she picked up the phone and dialed Michael's extension. "Mr. Lawrence, your sister-in-law, Ms. Emerson is here to see you. Yes, right away."

"Ms. Emerson. Please go right in," she told me.

"Thank you," I told her over my shoulder while walking down the hall to Michael's office. Michael was standing, waiting in the doorway for me. We gave each other a quick hug and kiss before I sat down. Michael was really cute in a very, very nerdy way. He was tall and thin, with nice large hazel colored eyes, but he wore wire rimmed eyeglasses, bow ties, fisherman-style hats; and he was shy. It might have been a good look on someone else or a senior citizen, but on him he just looked like a nerd. Jackie adored how he looked, and he adored her. I had to find out what was going on.

"Good morning Michael." I said but my sweet smile was gone, I was here for business.

"Good morning Ev; can I get you some coffee or something?" He asked me in a calm voice but he looked really nervous while he waited for my answer. He was rubbing his hands on his pants legs as if to dry his palms. Hmm, wet palms. Why I wondered.

"No thank you; I'm fine. I've had two cups already before I left the house. It's that husband of mine that never seems to be without a cup. I'm here to talk to you about Jackie."

"Uh, sure." He said, sitting down at his desk. "Have a seat." I noticed he wasn't looking me in my face, but at his hands.

"Michael, you know me," I said to him in a soothing tone, trying to convey I was there to give comfort. "Normally, I wouldn't intrude on someone's marriage but Jackie has been acting really out of character lately."

"Yes, I know." he said.

"Did she tell you what happened while we were away?" I asked him

"Yeah, she did," Michael said, sounding distraught and he looked it too. He looked like a man who's shipped had sailed and left him at the dock. The look on his face worried me a little.

"Michael, what is going on?"

"Jackie thinks I'm cheating on her, but I've never done anything like that or wanted to. I've loved Jackie and only her since I've met her, but she won't believe me and I don't know what to do. Her jealousy caused you so much trouble in Tennessee and now she won't get out of bed. I just don't know what to do."

The longer he talked the lower his voice had gotten; by the end I could barely hear him. He looked utterly crestfallen.

"Well, what about Yolanda, the assistant?" Bingo! As soon as I asked him that his entire body became rigid. He didn't lift his head though.

"What about her?" he asked me.

"Well, first of all, I've seen her; and though she seems very efficient at her job, she doesn't dress appropriately for an office environment. But that could be easily corrected. Why does Jackie believe you are having an affair with Yolanda?"

"Jackie is not comfortable around Yolanda, but I've never looked at Yolanda in any way other than as my assistant."

"So why did you seem to become uncomfortable when I asked you about her? And she seemed to become just as uncomfortable when I told her I was your sister-in-law. Why?"

"She likes me!" He said in a pleading tone. "But I swear I don't like her like that. But I can't let someone go just because they like me, especially when they're good at their job. We worked late for a couple of weeks when we were getting those files together on a large client that was being audited and she let me know how she felt. I did not reciprocate at all. I told her I was a happily married man and that's all."

He had of course given me this confession at the speed of light and now he looked exhausted and it was only nine-thirty in the morning. I felt sorry for him because I knew Michael was not cheating like I had always believed, but what had become obvious to me as he talked and I observed him: he was afraid of Yolanda, the sex temptress.

"What happened after you told her you weren't interested, how have things been?" I needed more information; I still didn't have a clear picture of the situation.

"Uh, well!" Michael was stalling and turning red under his very light complexion at the same time. "Well," he continued. "That's when she started dressing less, uh, professional, so I just stay and eat my lunch in here except when Jackie comes for our weekly lunch. She's really nice though, and does her job well."

"What do your associates say?" I asked, exasperated.

"They think she's nice and some say she's hot, but other than that I don't know. I didn't want to mention her clothes because I didn't want her to know that I noticed." He said this most sincerely. I couldn't believe this; Michael, a grown man in his forties was actually this clueless.

"Listen Michael, she knows you noticed. Just because you don't say anything doesn't make her think you haven't noticed. If she thought you didn't notice, she would go back to wearing appropriate attire. She has you hiding in your office for goodness sake." I had stood up and was leaning over his desk glaring down at him by this time.

"You don't know why Jackie thinks you're having an affair? Michael, come on! Give me a break! You've got Yolanda sex-goddess on the prowl, trying to wreck your marriage with my sister so she can have you."

Michael was sputtering now. "Bu, but I would never cheat on Jackie!"

"It doesn't matter if you would or not. Once she started changing her clothes for you to notice her, that was the signal to get her out of here. You have been married over twenty years so you know Jackie is not in the habit of accusing or suspecting these kinds of things."

"What grounds would I have had to fire her?"

"How about sexual harassment?" I challenged.

"That's a serious charge to put on someone's record. It follows you forever. I wouldn't want to do that!"

"You're right. It is a serious charge. But losing your marriage is serious as well, don't you think?" I asked him.

"But I'm not losing my marriage."

"Michael!" I cut him off. "Look at Jackie, look how she's been. Is she the same wife you've had all these years? I'm sure she's not because she's not even the same sister I've had." He now looked miserable and so he should, allowing that poison to stay in his office.

"Do you want Yolanda to stay?" I asked him, staring him straight in the eyes. I already knew what the answer was but I didn't want anyone saying it was my decision.

"No, of course not! But I just can't fire her without cause. She won't have an income."

Michael was a good guy, too good actually. He still cared that he did the right thing even though his assistant was definitely not doing the right thing by him and Jackie.

"Well. Let me handle it. I promise I will take care of it; I'll be back after lunch. See you then!" I said as I left out his office.

Chapter Twenty Eight

I walked back into Michael's firm at one-thirty that afternoon but I was not alone; I had Adele with me, Mrs. Foster, and her daughter Sylvia Stillwell. Mrs. Foster had been my father's assistant from way back when, and I swear she was near a hundred years old but she refused to retire because she didn't want to be at home with her husband all day and they couldn't just let an institution go, so they kept her on, but hired her daughter Sylvia to *"assist"* her. They were currently Adele's assistants or rather formally. Yolanda the sextress was very surprised to see us all walk in the office.

"Hello again," I said, giving her a genuine smile this time. "Please call Mr. Michael Lawrence and have him come out here."

"Of course." She said and immediately picked up the phone and called Michael.

"Yolanda, I would like to introduce you to my sister Adele Edwards. She is an attorney in our law firm upstairs, and this is Mrs. Foster and her daughter Sylvia Stillwell." Yolanda shook each of their hands and smiled sweetly to convey an air of calm, but I could see she was nervous and wondering why we were here and why I was introducing them to her.

Michael joined us with a questioning look on his face.

"Michael," I said as he walked over to me. "Adele offered to have Yolanda come work for her so that you can have Mrs. Foster and Sylvia."

"What?!!!" Yolanda practically shouted facing Michael. "Mr. Lawrence, what's going on?" She was looking panicked now! The wench!

"Yolanda, please calm down." Adele said to her, looking stunning and in charge in her black three-piece pinstripe suit. "This is what's going to happen. Beginning tomorrow, you will work for me, and Mrs. Foster and Sylvia will work for Michael. Sylvia will train you and get you up to speed. Michael said you are an excellent administrative assistant, so I'm sure you will have no problem getting acclimated with how I do things." Adele said this all in a very no nonsense way; it told Yolanda without saying flat-out to get on board or get out.

"Why?" Yolanda asked close to tears. I don't know why she was crying. She still had a job, she just wouldn't be able to sexually harass my brother-in-law any longer or cause my sister any more pain or stress.

Adele sighed impatiently at Yolanda but proceeded to answer her. "This was a corporate business decision that we felt would better suit the needs of our companies. In reality, the law firm was not connected to Michael's accounting firm in any way; it was just in the same building. But Yolanda need not know that. Besides we were all family, and family stuck together. "The hours you will be working are eight to five," Adele continued. "You will have to change your style of dress; we're a law firm, and the dress code is business professional. As I said before, Sylvia will get you up to speed so she will meet you in the morning. I'm going directly to court so I will see you after. See you tomorrow," She said and then left out the door with a wave.

"Yolanda, please show Sylvia and Mrs. Foster around the office and get them up to speed with things," I told her. "I have to leave now but I'll stop in next week to see how everyone is doing. Michael, I know you're busy." I didn't know any such thing and didn't care. "But why don't you leave early today and spend some time your *wife*." I said wife with emphasis so that Yolanda was clear on who Michael belonged to and where he was going to stay.

"I think that is a good idea." Michael said. "I will just get my things and head on home."

I bid them all a good day and I turned and left.

* * * *

The rest of the week I got back into the swing of things and returned to work, it was now Saturday and all of my sisters were coming over for the evening. No sister-in-laws though, just us Isaacs women. I hadn't talked much with my sisters in the past week since we'd been back home, and though I was anxious to get rid of them at the time, I was more than ready to see them now.

I was in my bedroom getting dressed in jeans and sweater when I heard a knock on my door. "Come in!" I called. The door opened and to my shock they were all at my door.

"Okay! This is weird!" I said.

"May we come in?" Jackie asked.

"Of course you may. You know better than to have to ask, and I already said come in. Sit down." I told them. They all filed in one after the other and sat down on my bed.

"So what do I owe the pleasure of your visit to my bedroom?" I asked jokingly. Everyone turned their heads to look at Jackie, who in turn stood up, walked away towards my seating area then turned around to face us. She wasn't smiling and instead looked a bit sad.

"I want to apologize to all of you for all that I put everyone through in Tennessee. I would never intentionally do anything to hurt any of you." Jackie started crying like I knew she would.

"Jackie, it's over and we're fine, you..." I started to interrupt but she held up her hand and stopped me.

"No Evelyn, I do have to. I love you all so much and you all risked everything for me, because of me. I'm just so sorry. Would you all forgive me?"

I turned and looked at my sisters and they looked right back at me. "What do you say; should we forgive her?" Gwen asked. We were still silent and as I looked at Jackie she was actually worried. I could see it all over her face and her body language showed it as well, as she rubbed her hand over the cast on her other hand repeatedly.

"Jackie! How can you even ask us if we forgive you?" Ava asked. "I believe we all forgave you in the chalet as Evelyn was coming up with the crazy plan. We're your sisters and we love you just as much as you love us! Now stop all that crying." We were all smiling at her by this time and she finally smiled back.

"You guys are the best sisters in the world." Jackie said as I actually saw the stress leave her face and body.

"And don't you forget it!" We all said to her and burst out laughing.

"Adele, what happened with Anne's divorce situation?" Jackie asked.

"I'm handling that!" Gwen said. "And he was served yesterday morning with the papers. I'll be seeing him in court and I'm looking forward to it."

"I wanted you all to know." Jackie spoke up again. "I went to the doctor and apparently I'm going into early menopause and that was the main reason for my extreme emotions or my lack of controlling my extreme emotions."

"At your age!?" Adele asked incredulous at the thought.

"Yes, I was shocked as well but I'm glad that I know it's menopause and not me going crazy instead."

"Well, I suppose if you put it like that." Adele said and we laughed some more.

"Adele, you never told us what you did to get that deputy to hightail it out of the sheriff's department so fast. What did you do?" Gwen asked

"After we drove back to the resort, I had Katherine park in a spot near the exit. I got out and walked around to the front of the building. When I got there, I saw both patrol cars and saw that there was no one near them. I felt bad for what I knew I had to do. We had already broken so many laws already that I concluded a few more wouldn't make much more of a difference." Adele paused looking very guilty in light of what she had done. I could tell that though she was explaining it in a voice of indifference I knew better. She felt bad.

"Sooo?" Ava asked her. "What did you do?"

"You know how I always keep a lighter on me. I don't know why, just out of habit for some reason. I took off my extra pair of socks, lit them on fire and put them under the seat in the patrol car. It took a minute for the fire to actually ignite into flames but there was tons of smoke. Once I saw that someone noticed and had run into the resort to report it, I figured they would call the other deputy to come. And they did, just as I thought they would."

"Wow!" we all said in unison.

"How do you feel?" I asked her.

"I'm fine and hungry, so let's all go downstairs so we can eat. I brought plenty of money for poker afterwards; I plan to wipe the floor with you;" Adele said grinning. I knew she was far from fine as she stated but we would get no more from her on the subject, at least not then; we knew we had to let it go.

We all agreed we were starving and indeed more than ready to eat and take up Adele's challenge for poker. As I followed them out of my bedroom, the strangest thought occurred to me. I can't believe all of this happened because of menopause!

The End

If you enjoyed this book, please don't forget to leave a review and share it with your friends on Facebook, Goodreads, Twitter, and wherever you purchased it.

Read excerpt from the second book in the series

Pulled In Again - An Evelyn Lee Emerson Novel

HOUSTON! Had I just heard my mother correctly? She had just informed us that we not only had to go to a funeral in Houston. But me and Jackie had to stay down there afterwards, and get our second cousin once removed or some such nonsense house cleared up and ready for sell.

"Mama, what did you just say?" I asked my mother in disbelief. This is what I get for having Sunday dinner with my family, at my parents' home. I should have stayed home and had my own dinner, in my own house.

"Well, you know your cousin Roberta's husband just died and we need to go down there for the funeral. She's too old to do the work herself so I told her you and Jackie would stay down there and help her." My mother stated as if what she had just signed us up for, without first asking, was how you treated your adult daughters.

The entire dining room had gone quiet, waiting to see how this would play out. There was a huge audience since all my brothers and sisters were there with their corresponding spouses. Adding Mama and Daddy, that made sixteen counting myself. Everyone's eyes were going back and forth between me, who sat at one end to the left of my daddy, who sat at the head of the table. Jackie, who was somewhere in the middle on my side, and to my mama who sat all the way at the other end, opposite daddy.

"Why didn't you ask us first?" Jackie asked, quietly, but I could tell she was upset.

"I don't see what the big deal is. We're family and family helps when another family member is in need." Mama replied in the most innocent of tones.

"Then why didn't' you volunteer yourself?" Jackie challenged.

My mother looked at Jackie as if she had just sprouted another head. "Me?" My mother asked indignantly. "It's too hot down there for me! I'm going to the funeral, then I'm getting right back on the plane and coming back." She said, then took another drink of lemonade from her glass.

I glanced over at Jackie and I could practically see the steam rising from her ears. I would love to say I couldn't believe what my mother just said, but in fact I could. This was my mother, Patricia Isaacs, the queen of entitlement.

"We barely know these people, and you expect us to not only go to the funeral but to clean up their house too!" Jackie's voice was starting to sound shrill. If this went on much longer she would be crying and screaming at the same time. And my mother would ignore her and pass it off as a "Jackie moment". I had to step in and say something, not one of my loving family members would come to our rescue. That included Tony, my husband, Michael, Jackie's husband or Daddy. The wimps!

"Uh Mama, doesn't Roberta have children, or even grandchildren that can help her? And why does she need her house cleared up anyway?" I asked, trying to interject calmness back into the situation, though I was just as ticked off as Jackie. I just wasn't as emotional.

"Yes, she does have two daughters but they have to work. I didn't ask about her grandchildren, she mentioned she didn't know how she was going to get it done and I thought of you two."

"But Mama, we have busy lives and I have my own business to run!" My mother knew this but I suppose she needed reminding. "And you could have just as easily volunteered Ava, Adele or Gwen." I added.

Adele, who sat directly across from me kicked me under the table for offering up her name to my mother, to be put on the chopping block with us.

"Oh poo," Mama said, waiving her hand in a dismissive gesture at my offer. "Jackie doesn't work, and your office doesn't need you. The girls can handle things just fine while you're away." The girls, she was referring to were my daughter Alicia, and my daughter-in-law Mia, who worked for me. They could, in fact run the office just perfectly in my absence, but it was the principle of the matter. And Jackie didn't have a job but she worked all the time. She volunteered, chaired all sorts of charity events, and sat on boards of one organization or another. My mother actually sat on some of the same boards, but obviously, none of that mattered right now because what she wanted, trumped all.

"And besides," Mama continued. "Your sisters are attorneys. They can't just miss court, that's too important."

I had to fight the urge and vision in my head, of taking the roll off my plate and sending it hurtling down the table to whack my mother in the head with it.

Now, this I couldn't believe. My mother, was still holding it against me and Jackie that we hadn't gone to law school like everyone else! How many attorneys did one family need?

"Mama, everyone here can take off from work. You know why? We all work for ourselves. Yes, Ava, Gwen, and Adele are lawyers, but there are other associates who can take their cases if need be." I said, getting a bit huffed myself by this time.

"Once you and Jackie get acclimated with things down there, I'm sure you and she will be just fine." Mama stated, then going back to her plate of food. Apparently, I was having an "Evelyn moment" to her, since she obviously, and easily dismissed what I had just said as well.

"Can't we just hire movers for her?" Jackie said, a little calmer now.

"Nooooo," my mother replied as if talking to a petulant child drawing out her words. "We cannot. Roberta has been in that house for more than twenty years, maybe even thirty, and all of that stuff needs to be gone through first. Then either thrown away or packed up. You can't leave that job up to some movers that wouldn't care about her mementos. You can have movers pack everything, once you've gone through it with her, but only after that."

I didn't care about them either, I thought but did not say. "And why are we clearing, and packing, or whatever else anyway? You never said." I asked her.

"Oh, we're moving her here. I thought I had mentioned that. I've already found her a wonderful apartment for seniors. I'll have it all decorated, and furnished for when she gets here. So no need to keep any furniture, unless she has a favorite chair, or something like that she wants to keep. The funeral is this Saturday, so be sure you let everyone know you'll both be gone for a couple of weeks." My mother was apparently finished discussing this with us and I had resigned myself to the fact that I was on my way to Houston, Texas.

About the Author

Denise Jewell was born and raised in Cincinnati, Ohio where she resided until 2011 when she decided to pray and take her chances. She packed up and moved herself and daughter to Houston, Texas where she has resided since. Happy with her move she continued her career in the medical insurance field. She is an avid reader and lover of mystery dinner theaters and manages to find one to attend everywhere she visits, time permitting, sometimes traveling to the city just to experience the theater. She desires to travel all over the world, from the smallest of towns to the largest of the big cities. The characters in her stores are real to her and having been swimming around in her mind for years and after a shove from her daughter she took the plunge and took them from her head to paper.

You may contact Denise at these following sites.
Website @ DeniseJewell.com
Facebook @ denisejewell-author
Twitter @denisejewell72
Goodreads @ denise_jewell

TRADEMARKS AND ACKNOWLEDGMENT

This author acknowledges the trademark status and trademark owners of the following wordmarks mentioned in this work of fiction:

BMW-BMW
Oil of Olay-Proctor and Gamble
Cadillac Escalade-General Motors
Hummer-General Motors
Cartier-Compagnie Financiere Richemont SA
Valentino-Marzotto Apparel
IPOD-Apple Inc
Facebook-Facebook Inc
The Andy Griffith Show-CBS Television Distribution
Alice-Warner Bros-Television
She's A Bad Mama Jama-written by Leon Haywood, sung by Carl Carlton